BEST LOVED BOOKS
FOR YOUNG READERS

Treasure Island

A CONDENSATION OF THE BOOK BY

Robert Louis Stevenson

Illustrated by Louis S. Glanzman

CHOICE PUBLISHING, INC.

New York

PRODUCED IN ASSOCIATION WITH MEDIA PROJECTS INCORPORATED

Executive Editor, Carter Smith
Managing Editor, Jeanette Mall
Project Editor, Jacqueline Ogburn
Associate Editor, Charles Wills
Contributing Editor, Edith Austin
Art Director, Bernard Schleifer

Library of Congress Catalog Number: 88-63362
ISBN: 0-945260-23-7

This 1989 edition is published and distributed by Choice Publishing, Inc.,
Great Neck, NY 11021, with permission of The Reader's Digest Association, Inc.

Manufactured in the United States of America.

10 9 8 7 6 5 4 3 2

OTHER TITLES IN THE

Reader's Digest

BEST LOVED BOOKS
FOR YOUNG READERS
SERIES

The Adventures of Tom Sawyer by Mark Twain
The Merry Adventures of Robin Hood by Howard Pyle
Alice's Adventures in Wonderland and
      Through the Looking Glass by Lewis Carroll
Great Cases of Sherlock Holmes by Sir Arthur Conan Doyle
Tales of Poe by Edgar Allan Poe
Little Women by Louisa May Alcott
The Jungle Books by Rudyard Kipling
The Life and Strange Surprising Adventures of Robinson Crusoe
      by Daniel Defoe
The Call of the Wild by Jack London and
      Typhoon by Joseph Conrad
Twenty Thousand Leagues Under the Sea by Jules Verne
The Adventures of Huckleberry Finn by Mark Twain
The Story of King Arthur and His Knights by Howard Pyle
Kidnapped by Robert Louis Stevenson
Beau Geste by Percival Christopher Wren
The Red Badge of Courage by Stephen Crane

Foreword

IN THE SCOTTISH HIGHLANDS one summer day, Robert Louis Stevenson and his stepson were confined to their cottage by rain. To amuse the boy Stevenson started to sketch the hills and harbors and brooks of a fancied island, and as he did so the idea of *Treasure Island* was born.

"The future characters of the book began to appear there visibly among the imaginary woods," he wrote later. "Their brown faces and bright weapons peeped out upon me from unexpected quarters as they passed to and fro, fighting and hunting treasure. . . . The next thing I knew I had some papers before me and was writing out a list of chapters."

The "list of chapters" soon became one of the world's most famous adventure stories. "Will you be surprised," Stevenson wrote a friend, "to learn that it is about buccaneers and treasure, and a mutiny, and a derelict ship, and a sea-cook with one leg, and a sea-song with the chorus 'Yo-ho-ho and a bottle of rum'?"

His friends may well have been surprised, for although Stevenson had been writing for some years, *Treasure Island* was his first successful novel. It was followed by *The Black Arrow, Kidnapped, The Strange Case of Dr. Jekyll and Mr. Hyde*, and the much beloved *A Child's Garden of Verses*, among many other books.

Toward the end of his life, yet still as adventurous in spirit as any of his fictional heroes, Stevenson fled the cold and the damp mists of Scotland for the South Seas, settling in Samoa. The Samoans revered the man they called *Tusitala*—teller of tales. When at the age of forty-four he died, they honored his wish and buried him high on Mount Vaea, "under the wide and starry sky." On his gravestone they inscribed the last lines of the beautiful poem he called "Requiem":

> Here he lies where he longed to be;
> Home is the sailor, home from the sea,
> And the hunter home from the hill.

1. THE OLD SEA DOG
AT THE ADMIRAL BENBOW

Squire Trelawney, Dr. Livesey and the rest of these gentlemen having asked me to write down the whole particulars about Treasure Island, from the beginning to the end, keeping nothing back but the bearings of the island, and that only because there is still treasure not yet lifted, I take up my pen in the year of grace 17—, and go back to the time when my father kept the Admiral Benbow inn, and the brown old seaman with the saber cut first took up his lodging under our roof.

I remember him as if it were yesterday as he came plodding to the inn door, his sea chest following behind him in a handbarrow; a tall, strong, heavy, nut-brown man; his tarry pigtail falling over the shoulders of his soiled blue coat; his hands ragged and scarred, with black, broken nails; and the saber cut across one cheek, a dirty, livid white. I remember him looking round the cove and whistling to himself as he did so, and then breaking out in that old sea song that he sang so often afterward:

> *"Fifteen men on the Dead Man's Chest—*
> *Yo-ho-ho, and a bottle of rum!"*

in the high old tottering voice that seemed to have been tuned and broken at the capstan bars. Then he rapped on the door with a bit of a stick like a handspike that he carried, and, when my father appeared,

I

called roughly for a glass of rum. This, when it was brought to him, he drank slowly, like a connoisseur, lingering on the taste and still looking about him at the cliffs and up at our signboard.

"This is a handy cove," says he, at length; "and a pleasant sittyated grogshop. Much company, mate?"

My father told him no, very little company, the more was the pity.

"Well, then," said he, "this is the berth for me. Here you, matey," he cried to the man who trundled the barrow, "bring up alongside and help up my chest. I'll stay here a bit," he continued. "I'm a plain man; rum and bacon and eggs is what I want, and that head up there for to watch ships off. What you mought call me? You mought call me Captain. Oh, I see what you're at—there"; and he threw down three or four gold pieces on the threshold. "You can tell me when I've worked through that," says he, looking as fierce as a commander.

And, indeed, bad as his clothes were, and coarsely as he spoke, he had none of the appearance of a man who sailed before the mast; but seemed like a mate or skipper, accustomed to be obeyed or to strike. The man who came with the barrow told us the mail had set him down the morning before at the "Royal George"; that he had inquired what inns there were along the coast, and hearing ours well spoken of, I suppose, and described as lonely, had chosen it from the others for his place of residence. And that was all we could learn of our guest.

He was a very silent man by custom. All day he hung round the cove, or upon the cliffs, with a brass telescope; all evening he sat in a corner of the parlor next the fire, and drank rum and water very strong. Mostly he would not speak when spoken to; only look up sudden and fierce, and blow through his nose like a foghorn; and we and the people who came about our house soon learned to let him be. Every day, when he came back from his stroll, he would ask if any seafaring men had gone by along the road. At first we thought it was the want of company of his own kind that made him ask this question, but at last we began to see he was desirous to avoid them. When a seaman put up at Admiral Benbow (as now and then some did, making by the coast road for Bristol), he would look in at him through the curtained door before he entered the parlor; and he was always as silent as a mouse when any such was present. For me, at least, there was no secret about the matter; for I was, in a way, a sharer in his alarms. He had taken me aside one day, and promised me a silver fourpenny on the first of every month if I would only keep my "weather eye open for a seafaring man with one leg." Often enough, when I applied to him for my wage, he would only blow through his nose and stare me down; but before the week was out, he was sure to think better of it, bring me my fourpenny piece, and repeat his orders to look out for "the seafaring man with one leg."

How that personage haunted my dreams, I need scarcely tell you. On stormy nights, when the wind shook the four corners of the house, and the surf roared along the cove and up the cliffs, I would see him in a thousand forms, with a thousand diabolical expressions; and to see him leap and run and pursue me over hedge and ditch was the worst of nightmares. But of the captain himself I was far less afraid than anybody else who knew him. There were nights when he took a deal more rum and water than his head would carry; and then he would sit and sing his wicked, old, wild sea songs, minding nobody; but sometimes he would call for glasses round, and slap his hand on the table for silence and force all the trembling company to bear a chorus to his singing. Often I have heard the house shaking with "Yo-ho-ho, and a bottle of rum," all the neighbors joining in for dear life, and each singing louder than the other, to avoid remark.

His stories were what frightened people worst of all. Dreadful stories they were, about hanging, and walking the plank, and storms at sea, and the Dry Tortugas, and wild deeds and places on the Spanish Main. By his own account he must have lived his life among some of the wickedest men that God ever allowed upon the sea; and the language in which he told these stories shocked our plain country people as much as the crimes that he described.

He was only once crossed, and that was toward the end, when my poor father was far gone in the decline that took him off. Dr. Livesey came late one afternoon to see the patient, took a bit of dinner from my mother, and went into the parlor to smoke a pipe. I followed him in, and I remember observing the contrast the neat, bright doctor, with his powder as white as snow, and his bright, black eyes and pleasant manners, made with that filthy, heavy, bleared pirate of ours, sitting far gone in rum, with his arms on the table. Suddenly he— the captain, that is—began to pipe up his eternal song:

> *"Fifteen men on the Dead Man's Chest—*
> *Yo-ho-ho, and a bottle of rum!*
> *Drink and the devil had done for the rest—*
> *Yo-ho-ho, and a bottle of rum!"*

At first I had supposed "the dead man's chest" to be that identical big box of his upstairs in the front room, the great sea chest none of us had ever seen open; and the thought had been mingled in my nightmares with that of the one-legged seafaring man. But by this time we had all long ceased to pay any particular notice to the song; it was new, that night, to nobody but Dr. Livesey, and on him I observed it did not produce an agreeable effect, for he looked up for a moment quite angrily before he went on with his talk to old Taylor, the gardener, on a new cure for the rheumatics. At last the captain flapped his hand upon the table for silence. The voices stopped at once, all but Dr. Livesey's; he went on as before, speaking clear and kind, and drawing briskly at his pipe between every word or two. The captain glared at him for a while, flapped his hand again and broke out with a villainous low oath: "Silence, there, between decks!"

"Were you addressing me, sir?" says the doctor; and when the ruffian had told him, with another oath, that this was so, "I have only one thing to say to you, sir," replies the doctor, "that if you keep on drinking rum, the world will soon be quit of a very dirty scoundrel!"

The old fellow's fury was awful. He sprang to his feet, drew and opened a sailor's clasp knife, and, balancing it open on the palm of his hand, threatened to pin the doctor to the wall.

The doctor never so much as moved. He spoke to him, as before, over his shoulder, and in the same tone of voice; rather high, so that all the room might hear, but perfectly calm and steady: "If you do not put that knife this instant in your pocket, I promise, upon my honor, you shall hang at next assizes."

Then followed a battle of looks between them; but the captain soon knuckled under, put up his weapon, and resumed his seat, grumbling like a beaten dog.

"And now, sir," continued the doctor, "since I now know there's such a fellow in my district, you may count I'll have an eye upon you day and night. I'm not a doctor only; I'm a magistrate; and if I catch a breath of complaint against you, if it's only for a piece of incivility like tonight's, I'll take effectual means to have you hunted down and routed out of this. Let that suffice."

Soon after Dr. Livesey's horse was brought to the door, and he rode away; but the captain held his peace that evening, and for many evenings to come.

IT WAS NOT VERY long after this that there occurred the first of the mysterious events that rid us at last of the captain, though not, as you will see, of his affairs. It was a bitter-cold winter, with long hard frosts and heavy gales; and it was plain from the first that my poor father was little likely to see the spring. He sank daily, and my mother and I had all the inn upon our hands, and were kept busy enough, without paying much regard to our unpleasant guest.

It was one January morning, very early, the sun still low and only touching the hilltops and shining far to seaward. The captain had risen earlier than usual, and set out down the beach, his cutlass swinging under the old blue coat, his brass telescope under his arm. I remember his breath hanging like smoke in his wake as he strode off.

Well, Mother was upstairs with Father, and I was laying the breakfast table, when the parlor door opened and a man stepped in on whom I had never set my eyes before. He was a pale, tallowy creature, wanting two fingers of the left hand; and, though he wore a cutlass, he did not look much like a fighter. He sat down upon a table and beckoned to me. I paused where I was, with my napkin in my hand.

"Come here, sonny," says he; "come nearer here."

I took a step nearer.

"Is this here table for my mate Bill?" he asked, with a kind of leer.

I told him I did not know his mate Bill; and this was for a person who stayed in our house, whom we called the captain.

"Well," said he, "my mate Bill would be called the captain, as like as not. We'll put it, for argument like, that your captain has a cut on his cheek—and we'll put it that that cheek's the right one. Now, is my mate Bill in this here house?" I told him he was out walking.

"Which way, sonny? Which way is he gone?"

And when I had pointed out the rock and told him how the captain was likely to return, and how soon, "Ah," said he, "this'll be as good as drink to my mate Bill."

The stranger hung about just outside the inn door, peering round the corner like a cat waiting for a mouse. Once I stepped outside myself, but he immediately called me back, and, as I did not obey quick enough for his fancy, a most horrible change came over his face, and he ordered me in with an oath that made me jump. As soon as I was back he returned to his former manner, patted me on the shoulder, told me I was a good boy, and he had taken quite a fancy to me.

"And here, sure enough," said he, "is my mate Bill, with a spyglass under his arm, bless his 'art to be sure. You and me'll just get behind the door, sonny, and we'll give Bill a little surprise."

So saying, the stranger backed along with me into the parlor, and put me behind him in the corner, so that we were both hidden by the open door. I was very uneasy and alarmed, as you may fancy, and it rather added to my fears to observe that the stranger was certainly frightened himself. He cleared the hilt of his cutlass and loosened the blade in the sheath.

At last in strode the captain, slammed the door behind him, without looking to the right or left, and marched straight across the room to where his breakfast awaited him.

"Bill," said the stranger, in a voice that I thought he had tried to make bold and big.

The captain spun round on his heel; all the brown had gone out of his face, and he had the look of a man who sees a ghost.

"Come, Bill, you know an old shipmate, surely," said the stranger.

The captain made a sort of gasp. "Black Dog!" said he.

"And who else?" returned the other. "Black Dog as ever was, come for to see his old shipmate Bill. Ah, Bill, we have seen a sight of times, us two, since I lost them two talons," holding up his mutilated hand.

"Now look here," said the captain, "you've run me down; well, then, speak up: what is it?"

"That's you, Bill," returned Black Dog, "you're in the right of it, Billy. I'll have a glass of rum, and we'll sit down and talk square like old shipmates."

When I returned with the rum they were already seated at the captain's table—Black Dog next to the door, sitting sideways, so as to have one eye on his old shipmate, and one, as I thought, on his retreat.

He bade me go, and leave the door wide open. "None of your keyholes for me, sonny," he said; and I retired into the bar.

For a long time, though I certainly did my best to listen, I could hear nothing; but at last the voices began to grow higher, and I could pick up a word or two, mostly oaths, from the captain. "No, no, no, no; and an end of it!" he cried once. And again, "If it comes to swinging, swing all, say I." Then all of a sudden there was a tremendous explosion of oaths, the chair and table went over in a lump, a clash of steel followed, and then a cry of pain, and the next instant I saw Black Dog in full flight, and the captain hotly pursuing, both with drawn cutlasses, and the former streaming blood from the left shoulder. Just at the door the captain aimed at the fugitive one last tremendous cut, which would certainly have split him to the chin had it not been intercepted by our big signboard of Admiral Benbow. You may see the notch on the frame to this day.

Once out upon the road, Black Dog, in spite of his wound, showed a wonderful clean pair of heels, and disappeared over the edge of the hill in half a minute. The captain, for his part, passed his hand over his eyes several times, and at last turned back into the house.

"Jim," says he, "rum"; and as he spoke he reeled a little, and caught himself with one hand against the wall.

"Are you hurt?" cried I.

"Rum," he repeated. "I must get away from here. Rum! rum!"

I ran to fetch it; but I was quite unsteadied by all that had fallen out, and I broke one glass and fouled the tap, and while I was still getting in my own way I heard a loud fall in the parlor and, running in, beheld the captain lying full length upon the floor. At the same instant my mother came running downstairs to help me. Between us we raised his head. He was breathing very loud and hard; but his eyes were closed and his face a horrible color.

"Dear, deary me!" cried my mother, "what a disgrace upon the house! And your poor father sick!"

In the meantime we had no idea what to do to help the captain, nor any other thought but that he had got his death-hurt in the scuffle with the stranger. I got the rum, to be sure, and tried to put it down his throat; but his teeth were tightly shut, and his jaws as strong as iron. It was a happy relief for us when the door opened and Dr. Livesey came in on his visit to my father.

"Oh, Doctor," we cried, "what shall we do? Where is he wounded?"

"Wounded? A fiddlestick's end!" said the doctor. "The man has had a stroke, as I warned him. Now, Mrs. Hawkins, just you run upstairs to your husband, and tell him, if possible, nothing about it. For my part, I must do my best to save this fellow's trebly worthless life; and Jim here will get me a basin."

When I got back the doctor had already ripped up the captain's sleeve and exposed his great sinewy arm. It was tattooed—"Here's luck," "A fair wind," and "Billy Bones his fancy"—on the forearm; and up near the shoulder there was a sketch of a gallows and a man hanging from it—done, as I thought, with great spirit.

"And now, Master Billy Bones, if that be your name," said the doctor, "we'll have a look at the color of your blood. Jim," he said, "are you afraid of blood?"

"No, sir," said I.

"Well, then," said he, "you hold the basin."

A great deal of blood was taken before the captain opened his eyes and looked mistily about him. First he recognized the doctor with an unmistakable frown; then his glance fell upon me, and he looked relieved. But suddenly his color changed, and he tried to raise himself, crying: "Where's Black Dog?"

"There's no Black Dog here," said the doctor, "except what you have on your own back. You have been drinking rum; you have had a stroke, precisely as I told you, and I have just dragged you head foremost out of the grave. Now, Mr. Bones—"

"That's not my name," he interrupted.

"Much I care," returned the doctor. "What I have to say to you is this: one glass of rum won't kill you, but if you take one you'll take another and another, and I stake my wig if you don't break off short you'll die—do you understand that? Come, now, make an effort. I'll help you to your bed for once."

Between us, with much trouble, we managed to hoist him upstairs, and laid him on his bed.

"Now, mind you," said the doctor, "I clear my conscience—the name of rum for you is death." And with that he went off to see my father, taking me with him.

"This is nothing," he said, as soon as he had closed the door. "I have drawn enough blood to keep him quiet awhile; he should lie for a week where he is—that is the best thing for him and you; but another stroke would settle him."

II. THE BLACK SPOT

ABOUT NOON I STOPPED at the captain's door with some cooling drinks and medicines. He was lying very much as we had left him, only a little higher, and he seemed both weak and excited. "Jim," he said, "you're the only one here that's worth anything; and you know I've been always good to you. Never a month but I've given you a silver fourpenny. And now you see, mate, I'm pretty low, and deserted by all; and, Jim, you'll bring me one noggin of rum, now, won't you, matey?"

"The doctor—" I began.

"Doctors is all swabs," he broke in; "and that doctor there, why, what do he know about seafaring men? I been in places hot as pitch, and mates dropping round with Yellow Jack, and the blessed land a-heaving like the sea with earthquakes—and I lived on rum, I tell you. It's been meat and drink, and man and wife to me; and if I'm not to have my rum, now I'm a poor old hulk on a lee shore, my blood'll be on you, Jim, and that doctor swab"; and he ran on for a while with curses. "Look, Jim, how my fingers fidget," he continued, in the pleading tone. "I can't keep 'em still, not I. I haven't had a drop this blessed day. If I don't have a drain o' rum, Jim, I'll have the horrors; I seen some on 'em already. I seen old Flint in the corner there behind you, as plain as print; and if I get the horrors I'll raise Cain. Your doctor hisself said one glass wouldn't hurt me. I'll give you a golden guinea for a noggin, Jim."

He was growing more and more excited, and this alarmed me, for my father needed quiet; besides, I was reassured by the doctor's words, now quoted to me, and rather offended by the offer of a bribe.

"I want none of your money," said I, "but what you owe my father. I'll get you one glass, and no more."

When I brought it to him he seized it greedily and drank it out. "Ay, ay," said he, "that's some better, sure enough. And now, matey, did that doctor say how long I was to lie here in this old berth?"

"A week at least," said I.

"Thunder!" he cried. "A week! I can't do that; they'd have the black spot on me. The lubbers is going about to get the wind of me in this blessed moment; lubbers as couldn't keep what they got, and want to nail what is another's. But I'm not afraid on 'em. I'll shake out another reef, matey, and daddle 'em again."

As he was thus speaking he had risen from bed with great difficulty, holding to my shoulder with a grip that almost made me cry out. He paused when he had got into a sitting position on the edge. "That doctor's done me," he murmured. "My ears is singing. Lay me back."

Before I could help him he had fallen back to his former place, where he lay for a while silent.

"Jim," he said, at length, "that Black Dog's a bad un; but there's worse that put him on. Now, if I can't get away nohow, and they tip me the black spot, mind you, it's my old sea chest they're after; you get that doctor swab, and tell him to pipe all hands—magistrates and sich—and he'll lay 'em aboard at the Admiral Benbow—all old Flint's crew, all on 'em that's left. I was old Flint's first mate, I was, and I'm the on'y one as knows the place. He gave it me, when he lay a-dying, like as if I was to now, you see. But you won't peach unless they get the black spot on me, or unless you see that Black Dog again, or a seafaring man with one leg, Jim—him above all."

"But what is the black spot, Captain?" I asked.

"That's a summons, mate. But you keep your weather eye open, Jim, and I'll share with you equals, upon my honor."

He wandered a little longer, but soon after I had given him his medicine, which he took like a child, he fell into a heavy sleep. What I should have done had all gone well I do not know. But as things fell out, my poor father died quite suddenly that evening, which put all other matters on one side. Our natural distress, the arranging of the funeral, and all the work of the inn to be carried on in the meanwhile kept me so busy that I had scarcely time to think of the captain.

He got downstairs next morning, to be sure, and had his meals as usual, though he ate little, and had more, I am afraid, than his usual supply of rum, for he helped himself out of the bar and no one dared to cross him. On the night before the funeral he was as drunk as ever; and it was shocking in that house of mourning to hear him singing away at his ugly old sea song; but, weak as he was, we were all in fear of death for him, for his temper was more violent than ever. He had an alarming way now, when he was drunk, of drawing his cutlass and laying it bare before him on the table. But, with all that, he minded people less, and seemed shut up in his own thoughts.

So things passed until the day after the funeral. That afternoon

I was standing at the door for a moment, full of sad thoughts, when I saw someone drawing near along the road. He was plainly blind, for he tapped before him with a stick and wore a great green shade over his eyes; and he was hunched and wore a huge old tattered sea cloak with a hood, that made him appear positively deformed. I never saw a more dreadful-looking figure. He stopped a little from the inn, and, in an odd singsong, addressed the air in front of him:

"Will any kind friend inform a poor blind man, who has lost the precious sight of his eyes in the gracious defense of his native country, England—and God bless King George!—where or in what part of this country he may now be?"

"You are at the Admiral Benbow, Black Hill Cove," said I.

"I hear a voice," said he, "a young voice. Will you give your hand, my kind young friend, and lead me in?" I held out my hand, and the horrible creature gripped it like a vise and pulled me close with a single action of his arm. "Now, boy," he said, "take me in to the captain."

"Sir," said I, "upon my word I dare not."

"Oh," he sneered, "that's it! Take me straight or I'll break your arm." And he gave it as he spoke a wrench that made me cry out.

"Sir," I said, "it is for yourself I mean. The captain sits with a drawn cutlass. Another gentleman—"

"Come, now, march," interrupted he; and I never heard a voice so cruel and cold as that blind man's. I began to obey him at once, walking straight in at the door and toward the parlor where our sick old buccaneer was sitting, dazed with rum. The blind man clung close to me, holding me in one iron fist. "Lead me straight to him, and when I'm in view cry out, 'Here's a friend for you, Bill.' If you don't, I'll do this"; and with that he gave me a fierce twitch. I was so utterly terrified of the blind beggar that I forgot my terror of the captain, and as I opened the parlor door cried out the words he had ordered.

The poor captain raised his eyes, and at one look the rum went out of him and left him staring sober. The expression of his face was not so much of terror as of mortal sickness.

"Now, Bill, sit where you are," said the beggar. "If I can't see,

I can hear a finger stirring. Business is business. Hold out your right hand. Boy, take his hand by the wrist, and bring it near to my right."

We both obeyed him to the letter, and I saw him pass something from the hollow of the hand that held his stick into the palm of the captain's, which closed upon it instantly.

"And now that's done," said the blind man; and at the words he suddenly left hold of me, and, with incredible accuracy and nimbleness, skipped out of the parlor and into the road, where I could hear his stick go tap-tap-tapping into the distance.

It was some time before either I or the captain seemed to gather our senses; but at length, and about at the same moment, I released his wrist, which I was still holding, and he drew in his hand and looked sharply into the palm.

"Ten o'clock!" he cried. "Six hours. We'll do them yet"; and he sprang to his feet. Even as he did so, he reeled, put his hand to his throat, stood swaying for a moment, and then, with a peculiar sound, fell from his whole height to the floor.

I ran to him at once, calling to my mother. But haste was all in vain. The captain had been struck dead by thundering apoplexy. It is a curious thing to understand, for I had certainly never liked the man, though of late I had begun to pity him, but as soon as I saw that he was dead I burst into a flood of tears. It was the second death I had known, and the sorrow of the first was still fresh in my heart.

III. THE SEA CHEST

I LOST NO TIME, of course, in telling my mother all that I knew, and we saw ourselves at once in a difficult and dangerous position. Some of the man's money—if he had any—was certainly due to us; but it was not likely that our captain's shipmates, above all the two specimens seen by me, Black Dog and the blind beggar, would be inclined to give up their booty in payment of the dead man's debts. The captain's order to ride at once for Dr. Livesey would have left my mother alone and unprotected, which was not to be thought of. Indeed, it seemed impossible for either of us to remain much longer in the house: what between the dead body of the captain on the parlor floor and the thought of that detestable blind beggar hovering near at hand, there were moments when, as the saying goes, I jumped in my skin for terror. It occurred to us at last to seek help in the neighboring hamlet. Bareheaded as we were, we ran out into the gathering evening and the frosty fog.

The hamlet lay not many hundred yards away, though out of view, on the other side of the next cove; and what greatly encouraged me, it was in an opposite direction from that whence the blind man had made his appearance and whither he had presumably returned. We were not many minutes on the road, but it was already candlelight when we reached the hamlet. I shall never forget how much I was cheered to see the yellow shine in doors and windows; but no soul, as it proved, would consent to return with us to the Admiral Benbow. The name of Captain Flint, though strange to me, carried a great weight of terror. Some of the men who had been to field work on the far side of the Admiral Benbow remembered, besides, to have seen several strangers on the road, and, taking them to be smugglers, to have bolted away; and one had seen a little lugger in what we called Kitt's Hole. The short and the long of the matter was, that while several were willing to ride to Dr. Livesey's, which lay in another direction, not one would help us to defend the inn.

When each had said his say my mother made them a speech. She would not, she declared, lose money that belonged to her fatherless boy. "If none of the rest of you dare," she said, "Jim and I dare. Back we will go, and small thanks to you big, hulking, chickenhearted men. We'll have that chest open if we die for it. And I'll thank you for that bag, Mrs. Crossley, to bring back our lawful money in."

Of course they all cried out at our foolhardiness; but even then not a man would go along with us. All they would do was to give me a loaded pistol lest we were attacked, and to promise to have horses ready saddled, in case we were pursued on our return; while one lad was to ride forward to the doctor's in search of armed assistance.

My heart was beating finely when we two set forth upon this dangerous venture. A full moon peered redly through the upper edges of the fog, and this increased our haste, for it was plain that our departure would be exposed to the eyes of any watchers. We slipped along the hedges, noiseless and swift, nor did we see or hear anything till the door of the Admiral Benbow had closed behind us.

I slipped the bolt, and in huge relief we stood and panted for a moment in the dark. Then my mother got a candle and, holding each other's hands, we advanced into the parlor. The dead captain lay as we had left him, with his eyes open and one arm stretched out.

"Draw down the blind, Jim," whispered my mother; "they might come and watch outside. And now," said she, when I had done so, "we have to get the key off *that;* and who's to touch it!" and she gave a kind of sob as she said the words.

I went down on my knees at once. On the floor close to his hand there was a little round of paper, blackened on the one side. I could not doubt that this was the black spot; and taking it up, I found written on the other side, in a very good clear hand, this short message: "You have till ten tonight."

"He had till ten, Mother," said I; and just as I said it our old clock began striking. This sudden noise startled us shockingly; but the news was good, for it was only six.

"Now, Jim," she said, "that key."

I felt in his pockets, but found only a few small coins, a thimble, some thread and big needles, a pocket compass, and a tinderbox. "Perhaps it's round his neck," suggested my mother. I tore open his shirt at the neck, and there, sure enough, hanging to a bit of tarry string, we found the key. At this we were filled with hope, and hurried up to the little room where his box had stood since the day of his arrival.

It was like any other seaman's chest on the outside, the initial "B." burned on the top with a hot iron, the corners somewhat broken.

"Give me the key," said my mother; and though the lock was stiff, she had turned it and thrown back the lid in a twinkling.

A smell of tobacco and tar rose from the interior, but nothing was to be seen on the top except a suit of very good clothes. Under that the miscellany began—a quadrant, a tin cannikin, several sticks of tobacco, two brace of handsome pistols, a piece of bar silver, an old Spanish watch, and other trinkets of little value and mostly of foreign make, and a pair of compasses mounted with brass.

Underneath there was an old boat cloak, whitened with sea salt. My mother pulled it up with impatience, and there lay before us the last things in the chest, a bundle tied up in oilcloth, and looking like papers, and a canvas bag that gave forth, at a touch, the jingle of gold.

"I'll show these rogues that I'm an honest woman," said she. "I'll have my dues, and not a farthing over." And she began to count over the amount of the captain's score from the sailor's bag.

It was a long, difficult business, for the coins were of all countries and sizes—doubloons, and louis-d'ors, and guineas, and pieces of eight, and I know not what besides, all shaken together at random. The guineas, too, were the scarcest, and it was with these only that my mother knew how to make her count.

When we were about halfway through I suddenly put my hand upon her arm; for I had heard a sound that brought my heart into my mouth—the tap-tapping of the blind man's stick upon the frozen road. It drew nearer while we sat holding our breath. Then it struck sharp on the inn door, and then we could hear the handle being turned, and the bolt rattling as the wretched being tried to enter; and then there was a long silence. At last the tapping recommenced, and, to our indescribable joy, died slowly away again.

"Mother," said I, "take the whole and let's be going." But my mother, frightened as she was, would not consent to take a fraction more than was due to her, and was obstinately unwilling to be content with less. It was not yet seven, she said, by a long way; she was still arguing with me when a little low whistle sounded a good way off upon the hill. That was enough for both of us.

"I'll take what I have," she said, jumping to her feet.

"And I'll take this to square the count," said I, picking up the oilskin packet.

Next moment we were both groping downstairs, leaving the candle by the empty chest; and the next we had opened the door and were in full retreat. The fog was rapidly dispersing; already the moon shone quite clear on the high ground on either side; and it was only on the exact bottom of the dell and round the tavern door that a thin veil still hung unbroken to conceal the first steps of our escape. Far less than halfway to the hamlet we must come forth into the moonlight. Nor was this all; for the sound of footsteps running came already to our ears, and as we looked back, a light tossing to and fro and rapidly advancing showed that one of the newcomers carried a lantern.

"My dear," said my mother, suddenly, "take the money and run on. I am going to faint."

This was certainly the end for both of us, I thought. How I cursed the cowardice of the neighbors; how I blamed my poor mother for her honesty and her greed!

We were just at the little bridge, by good fortune; and I helped her to the edge of the bank, where, sure enough, she gave a sigh and fell on my shoulder. I do not know how I found the strength, but I managed to drag her down and a little way under the arch. Farther I could not move her; so there we had to stay—within earshot of the inn.

But my curiosity was stronger than my fear; for I crept back to the bank again, whence I might command the road before our door. I was scarcely in position ere my enemies began to arrive, seven or eight of them, running hard, and the man with the lantern some paces in front. Three men ran together, hand in hand; and I made out, even through the mist, that the middle man of this trio was the blind beggar. The next moment his voice showed me that I was right.

"Down with the door!" he cried.

"Ay, ay, sir!" answered two or three; and a rush was made upon the Admiral Benbow. And then I could see them pause, as if they were surprised to find the door open. But the pause was brief, for the blind man again issued his commands.

"In, in!" he shouted, and cursed them for their delay.

Four or five of them obeyed at once, two remaining on the road with the formidable beggar. There was a pause, then a voice shouting from the house: "Bill's dead!"

The blind man swore at them again. "Search him, some of you shirking lubbers, and the rest aloft and get the chest."

I could hear their feet rattling up our old stairs. Promptly afterward fresh sounds of astonishment arose; the window of the captain's room was thrown open and a man leaned out into the moonlight and addressed the blind beggar below. "Pew," he cried, "someone's turned the chest out alow and aloft."

"Is it there?" roared Pew.

"The money's there."

The blind man cursed the money. "Flint's fist, I mean."

"We don't see it here nohow," returned the man.

"Here, you below there, is it on Bill?" cried Pew.

At that, another fellow came to the door of the inn. "Bill's been overhauled a'ready," said he, "nothin' left."

"It's these people of the inn—it's that boy. I wish I had put his eyes out!" cried the blind man, Pew. "They were here no time ago; they had the door bolted when I tried it. Scatter, lads, and find 'em."

Then there followed a great to-do through all our old inn, heavy feet pounding to and fro, furniture thrown over, doors kicked in, and the men came out, one after another, and declared that we were nowhere to be found. And just then the same whistle that had alarmed my mother and myself was once more clearly audible through the night, this time twice repeated. I had thought it to be the blind man summoning his crew to the assault; but I now found that it was a signal from the hillside toward the hamlet, and, from its effect upon the buccaneers, a signal to warn them of approaching danger.

"There's Dirk," said one. "We'll have to budge, mates."

"Budge, you skulk!" cried Pew. "They must be close by. Scatter and look for them, dogs! You have your hands on it. Oh, shiver my soul, he cried, "if I had eyes!"

This appeal seemed to produce some effect, for two of the fellows began to look here and there among the lumber, but the rest stood irresolute upon the road. "You have your hands on thousands, you fools, and you stand there malingering!" Pew went on. "There wasn't one of you dared face Bill, and I did it—a blind man! And I'm to lose my chance through you! I'm to be a poor, crawling beggar, sponging for rum, when I might be rolling in a coach!"

"Hang it, Pew, we've got the doubloons!" grumbled one.

"They might have hid the blessed thing," said another. "Take the Georges, Pew, and don't stand here squalling."

Squalling was the word for it, Pew's anger rose so high at these objections; till at last, his passion completely taking the upper hand, he struck at them right and left in his blindness, and his stick sounded heavily on more than one.

This quarrel was the saving of us; for while it was still raging, another sound came from the top of the hill on the side of the hamlet—the tramp of horses galloping. Almost at the same time a pistol shot, flash and report, came from the hedgeside. And that was plainly the last signal of danger; for the buccaneers turned at once and ran, disappearing in every direction. Pew they had deserted, whether in sheer panic or out of revenge for his ill words and blows, I know not; but there he remained behind, groping and tapping up and down the road in a frenzy, calling for his comrades. Finally he took the wrong turn, and ran a few steps past me, toward the hamlet, crying: "Johnny, Black Dog, Dirk—you won't leave old Pew, mates—not old Pew!"

Just then the noise of horses topped the rise, and four or five riders came in sight in the moonlight, and swept at full gallop down the slope. At this Pew saw his error, turned with a scream and ran, first off the road, and then, utterly bewildered, right under the nearest of the coming horses. The rider tried to save him, but in vain. Down went Pew with a cry that rang into the night; the four hoofs trampled him and passed by, and he moved no more.

I leaped to my feet and hailed the riders. They were pulling up at any rate, horrified at the accident. One was the lad that had gone from the hamlet to Dr. Livesey's; the rest were revenue officers, whom he had met by the way, and with whom he had returned at once. Some news of the lugger in Kitt's Hole had found its way to Supervisor Dance, and set him forth that night in our direction, and to that circumstance my mother and I owed our preservation from death.

Pew was dead, stone-dead. As for my mother, when we had carried her up to the hamlet she was none the worse for her terror. In the meantime the supervisor rode on to Kitt's Hole; but it was no surprise that when he got to the Hole the lugger was already under way. Mr. Dance hailed her. A voice replied, telling him to keep out of the moonlight or he would get some lead in him, and at the same time a bullet whistled close by his arm. Soon after the lugger doubled the point and disappeared.

I went with Mr. Dance to the Admiral Benbow, and you cannot imagine a house in such a state of smash; the very clock had been thrown down by these fellows in their furious hunt after my mother and myself; and though nothing had been taken except the captain's money bag and a little silver from the till, I could see at once that we were ruined. Mr. Dance could make nothing of the scene.

"They got the money, you say? Well, then, Hawkins, what in fortune were they after?"

"I believe I have the thing in my pocket," replied I, "and, to tell the truth, I should like to get it put in safety. I thought, perhaps, Dr. Livesey—"

"Perfectly right," he interrupted very cheerily, "perfectly right—a gentleman and a magistrate. And, now I come to think of it, I might as well ride round there myself and report to him or Squire. If you like, Hawkins, I'll take you along."

I thanked him heartily for the offer, and we walked back to the hamlet where the horses were. By the time I had told Mother of my purpose the men were all in the saddle.

"Dogger," said Mr. Dance, "you have a good horse: take up this lad behind you "

We rode hard all the way, till we drew up before Dr. Livesey's door. Mr. Dance told me to jump down and knock. The door was opened almost at once by the maid.

"Is Dr. Livesey in?" I asked.

No, she said; he had gone up to the Hall to dine with the squire.

"So there we go, boys," said Mr. Dance.

This time, as the distance was short, I did not mount, but ran with Dogger's stirrup leather to the lodge gates, and up the long leafless, moonlit avenue to where the white line of the Hall buildings looked on either hand on great old gardens. Here Mr. Dance dismounted and, taking me along with him, was admitted at a word into the house.

The servant showed us into a great library, all lined with bookcases and busts upon the top of them, where the squire and Dr. Livesey sat, pipe in hand, on either side of a bright fire.

I had never seen the squire so near at hand. He was a tall man, over six feet high, and broad in proportion, and he had a bluff, rough-and-ready face, all reddened and lined in his long travels. His eyebrows were black, and moved readily, and this gave him a look of some temper, not bad, you would say, but quick and hot.

"Come in, Mr. Dance," says he, very stately and condescending.

"Good evening, Dance," says the doctor, with a nod. "And good evening to you, Jim. What good wind brings you here?"

The supervisor stood up straight and stiff, and told his story like a lesson; and you should have seen how the two gentlemen leaned forward in their surprise and interest. When they heard how my mother went back to the inn, Dr. Livesey fairly slapped his thigh, and the squire cried "Bravo!" Long before it was done, Mr. Trelawney (that, you will remember, was the squire's name) had got up from his seat, and was striding about the room, and the doctor, as if to hear the better, had taken off his powdered wig, and sat there, looking very strange indeed with his own close-cropped, black poll.

At last Mr. Dance finished the story.

"Mr. Dance," said the squire, "you are a very noble fellow. And as for riding down that atrocious miscreant, I regard it as an act of virtue, sir, like stamping on a cockroach. This lad Hawkins is a trump, I perceive. Hawkins, will you ring that bell? Mr. Dance must have some ale."

"And so, Jim," said the doctor, "you have what they were after?"

"Here it is, sir," said I, and gave him the oilskin packet.

The doctor looked it all over, as if his fingers were itching to open it; but, instead, he put it in his coat pocket. "Squire," said he, "when Dance has had his ale he must, of course, be off on his Majesty's service; but I mean to keep Jim Hawkins here to sleep at my house, and, with your permission, I propose we should have up the cold pie, and let him sup." So a big pigeon pie was brought in and put on a side table, and I made a hearty supper while Mr. Dance was further complimented, and at last dismissed.

"And now, Squire," said the doctor.

"And now, Livesey," said the squire, in the same breath:

"One at a time, one at a time," laughed Dr. Livesey. "You have heard of this Flint, I suppose?"

"Heard of him!" cried the squire. "He was the bloodthirstiest buccaneer that sailed. Blackbeard was a child to Flint. The Spaniards were so prodigiously afraid of him that, I tell you, sir, I was sometimes proud he was an Englishman. I've seen his topsails with these eyes, off Trinidad, and the cowardly son of a rum puncheon that I sailed with put back—put back, sir, into Port of Spain."

"Well, I've heard of him myself, in England," said the doctor. "But the point is, had he money?"

"Money! What were these villains after but money?"

"That we shall soon know," replied the doctor. "But you are so confoundedly hotheaded and exclamatory that I cannot get a word in. What I want to know is this: Supposing that I have here in my pocket some clue to where Flint buried his treasure, will that treasure amount to much?"

"Amount, sir!" cried the squire. "It will amount to this; if we have the clue you talk about, I fit out a ship in Bristol dock, and take you and Hawkins here along, and I'll have that treasure if I search a year."

"Very well," said the doctor. "Now, then, we'll open the packet"; and he laid it before him on the table.

The bundle was sewn together, and the doctor had to get out his instrument case and cut the stitches with his medical scissors. It contained two things—a book and a sealed paper.

"First of all we'll try the book," observed the doctor.

The squire and I were both peering over his shoulder as he opened it. On the first page there were only some scraps of writing, such as a man might make for idleness or practice. One was the same as the tattoo mark—"Billy Bones his fancy"; then there were "Mr. W. Bones, mate"; "No more rum"; "Off Palm Key he got itt"; and some other snatches, mostly unintelligible.

"Not much instruction here," said Dr. Livesey.

The next ten or twelve pages were filled with a curious series of entries. There was a date at one end of the line and at the other a sum of money, as in common account books; but instead of explanatory writing, only a varying number of crosses between the two, and here and there a place name, as "Offe Caraccas." The record lasted over nearly twenty years, the amount of the separate entries growing larger as time went on, and at the end a grand total had been made out and these words appended, "Bones, his pile."

"I can't make head or tail of this," said Dr. Livesey.

"The thing is as clear as noonday," cried the squire. "This is the blackhearted hound's account book. These crosses stand for the names of ships or towns that they sank or plundered. The sums are the scoundrel's share, and where he feared an ambiguity, he added something clearer. 'Offe Caraccas,' now; you see, here was some unhappy vessel boarded off that coast. God help the poor souls that manned her—coral long ago."

"Right!" said the doctor. "And the amounts increase, you see, as he rose in rank."

There was little else in the volume but a few bearings of places noted in the blank leaves toward the end, and a table for reducing French, English, and Spanish moneys to a common value.

"Thrifty man!" cried the doctor. "He wasn't the one to be cheated."

"And now," said the squire, "for the other."

The paper had been sealed in several places with a thimble, by way of seal, the very thimble perhaps that I had found in the captain's pocket. The doctor opened the seals and there fell out the map of an island, with latitude and longitude, soundings, names of hills, and bays and inlets, and every particular that would be needed to bring a ship to a safe anchorage upon its shores. It was about nine miles long and five across, and there were marked two fine land-locked harbors, a house within a stockade, and a hill in the center marked "The Spye-glass." There were several additions of a later date; but, above all, three crosses of red ink—two on the north part of the island, one in the southwest, and, beside this last, in a small, neat hand very different from the captain's tottery characters, these words: "Bulk of treasure here."

Over on the back the same hand had written this further information:

Tall tree, Spye-glass shoulder, bearing a point to the N. of N.N.E.
Skeleton Island E.S.E. and by E.
Ten feet.
The bar silver is in the north cache; you can find it by the trend of the east hummock, ten fathoms south of the black crag with the face on it.
The arms are easy found, in the sand hill, N. point of north inlet cape, bearing E. and a quarter N.

J.F.

That was all; but, brief as it was, and, to me, incomprehensible, it filled the squire and Dr. Livesey with delight.

"Livesey," said the squire, "tomorrow I start for Bristol. In a few weeks' time we'll have the best ship, sir, and the choicest crew in England. Hawkins shall come as cabin boy. You, Livesey, are ship's doctor; I am admiral. We'll take Redruth, Joyce, and Hunter. We'll have not the least difficulty in finding the spot, and money to eat— to roll in—ever after."

"Trelawney," said the doctor, "I'll go with you; and, I'll go bail for it, so will Jim, and be a credit to the undertaking. There's only one man I'm afraid of."

"And who's that?" cried the squire. "Name the dog, sir!"

"You," replied the doctor; "for you cannot hold your tongue. We are not the only men who know of this paper. These fellows who attacked the inn tonight—and the rest who stayed aboard that lugger—are, one and all, bound that they'll get that money. We must none of us, from first to last, breathe a word of what we've found."

"Livesey," returned the squire, "you are always in the right of it. I'll be as silent as the grave."

IV. I GO TO BRISTOL

It was longer than the squire imagined ere we were ready for the sea. The doctor had to go to London for a physician to take charge of his practice; the squire was hard at work at Bristol; and I lived on at the Hall under the charge of old Redruth, the gamekeeper, full of sea dreams and the most charming anticipations of strange islands and adventures.

So the weeks passed on—till one fine day there came a letter addressed to Dr. Livesey, with this addition, "To be opened, in the case of his absence, by Tom Redruth, or young Hawkins." Obeying this order, we found, or rather I found—for the gamekeeper was a poor hand at reading anything but print—the following important news:

"Old Anchor Inn, Bristol, March 1, 17—

"Dear Livesey,—As I do not know whether you are at the Hall or still in London, I send this in double to both places.

"The ship is bought and fitted. She lies at anchor, ready for sea. You never imagined a sweeter schooner—a child might sail her—two hundred tons; name, *Hispaniola*.

"I got her through my old friend, Blandly, who has proved himself throughout the most surprising trump. The fellow literally slaved in my interest, and so, I may say, did everyone in Bristol, as soon as they got wind of the port we sailed for—treasure, I mean.

"Redruth," said I, interrupting the letter, "Dr. Livesey will not like that. The squire has been talking, after all."

"Well, who's a better right?" growled the gamekeeper. At that I gave up all commentary, and read straight on:

"So far there was not a hitch. The work-people, to be sure—riggers and what not—were most annoyingly slow; but it was the crew that troubled me. I wished a round score of men—in case of natives, buccaneers, or the odious French—and I had the worry of the deuce itself to find so much as half a dozen till a stroke of fortune brought me to the very man that I required.

"I was standing on the dock when by the merest accident I fell in talk with him. I found he was an old sailor, kept a public house, knew all the seafaring men in Bristol, had lost his health ashore, and wanted a good berth as cook to get to sea again. He had hobbled down there to get a smell of the salt. I was monstrously touched—so would you have been—and engaged him on the spot as ship's cook. Long John Silver, he is called, and has lost a leg; but that I regarded as a recommendation, since he lost it in his country's service under the immortal Hawke. He has no pension, Livesey. Imagine the abominable age we live in!

"Well, sir, I thought I had only found a cook, but it was a crew I had discovered. Between Silver and myself we got together in a few days a company of the toughest old salts imaginable—not pretty to look at, but fellows, by their faces, of the most indomitable spirit. I declare we could fight a frigate.

"Long John even got rid of two out of the six or seven I had already engaged. He showed me in a moment that they were just the freshwater swabs we had to fear in an adventure of importance.

"I am in the most magnificent health and spirits, yet I shall not enjoy a moment till I hear my old tarpaulins tramping round the capstan. Seaward ho! Hang the treasure! It's the glory of the sea that has turned my head. So now, Livesey, come post; do not lose an hour. Let young Hawkins go at once to see his mother, with Redruth for a guard; and then both come full speed to Bristol.

John Trelawney

"*Postscript*—I did not tell you that Blandly, who, by the way, is to send a consort after us if we don't turn up by the end of August, had found an admirable fellow for sailing master—a stiff man, which I regret, but in all other respects, a treasure. Long John Silver unearthed a very competent man for a mate, a man named Arrow. I have a boatswain who pipes, Livesey; so things shall go man-o'-war fashion on board the good ship *Hispaniola*.

"I forgot to tell you that Silver is a man of substance; I know of my own knowledge that he has a banker's account, which has never been overdrawn. He leaves his wife to manage the inn; and as she is a woman of color, a pair of old bachelors like you and I may be excused for guessing that it is the wife quite as much as the health that sends him back to roving.

J. T.

"*P.P.S.*—Hawkins may stay one night with his mother.

J. T."

You can fancy the excitement into which that letter put me. I was beside myself with glee; and if ever I despised a man it was old Tom Redruth, who could do nothing but grumble and lament.

The next morning he and I set out on foot for the Admiral Benbow, and there I found my mother in good health and spirits. The squire had had everything repaired, and the public rooms and the sign repainted, and had added some furniture—above all, a beautiful armchair for Mother in the bar. He had found her a boy as an apprentice also, so that she should not want help while I was gone.

It was on seeing that boy that I understood, for the first time, my situation. I had thought up to that moment of the adventures before me, not at all of the home I was leaving; and now at the sight of this clumsy stranger, who was to stay here in my place beside my mother, I had my first attack of tears. I am afraid I led that boy a dog's life; for he was new to the work, and I had a hundred opportunities of setting him right and putting him down.

The next day, after dinner, I said good-by to Mother, and Redruth and I were afoot again and on the road. The mail picked us up about dusk at the Royal George on the heath. I was wedged in between Redruth and a stout old gentleman, and in spite of the cold night air I must have slept like a log; for when I was awakened at last we were standing still in a city street, and day had already broken.

"Where are we?" I asked.

"Bristol," said Tom. "Get down."

Mr. Trelawney had taken up his residence at an inn far down the docks, to superintend the work upon the schooner. Thither we had now to walk, and our way, to my great delight, lay along the quays and beside the great multitude of ships of all sizes and rigs and nations. I saw the most wonderful figureheads that had all been far over the ocean. I saw, besides, many old sailors, with rings in their ears, and whiskers curled in ringlets, and tarry pigtails; and if I had seen as many kings I could not have been more delighted.

And I was going to sea myself; to sea in a schooner, with a piping boatswain, and pigtailed seamen; to sea, bound for an unknown island and to seek for buried treasures!

While I was still in this delightful dream we came in front of a large inn, and met Squire Trelawney, all dressed out like a sea officer, in stout blue cloth, coming out of the door with a smile on his face and a capital imitation of a sailor's walk.

"Here you are," he cried, "and the doctor came last night from London. Bravo! the ship's company complete!"

"Oh, sir," cried I, "when do we sail?"

"Sail!" says he. "We sail tomorrow!"

WHEN I HAD DONE breakfasting the squire gave me a note addressed to John Silver, at the sign of the Spy-glass, and told me I should easily find the place by following the line of the docks and keeping a lookout for a little tavern with a large brass telescope for a sign. I set off and picked my way among a great crowd of people and carts and bales until I found the tavern in question.

It was a bright enough little place. The sign was newly painted; the windows had neat red curtains; the floor was cleanly sanded. The customers were mostly seafaring men; and they talked so loudly that I hung at the door, almost afraid to enter.

As I was waiting, a man came out of a side room, and, at a glance, I was sure he must be Long John. His left leg was cut off close to the hip, and under the left shoulder he carried a crutch, which he managed with wonderful dexterity, hopping about upon it like a bird. He was very tall and strong, with a face as big as a ham—plain and pale, but intelligent and smiling. Indeed, he seemed in the most cheerful spirits, whistling as he moved about among the tables with a merry word or a slap on the shoulder for the more favored of his guests.

Now, to tell you the truth, from the very first mention of Long John in Squire Trelawney's letter, I had taken a fear in my mind that he might prove to be the very one-legged sailor whom I had watched for so long at the old Benbow. But one look at the man before me was enough. I had seen the captain, and Black Dog, and the blind man Pew, and I thought I knew what a buccaneer was like—a very different creature from this clean and pleasant-tempered landlord.

I plucked up courage, crossed the threshold, and walked right up to the man where he stood, propped on his crutch, talking to a customer. "Mr. Silver, sir?" I asked, holding out the note.

"Yes, my lad," said he, "such is my name. And who may you be?" And then as he saw the squire's letter, he seemed to give something like a start. "Oh!" said he, quite loud, and offering his hand, "I see. You are our new cabin boy; pleased I am to see you." And he took my hand in his large firm grasp.

Just then one of the customers rose and made for the door. It was close by him, and he was out in the street in a moment. But his hurry had attracted my notice, and I recognized him at a glance. It was the tallow-faced man, wanting two fingers, who had come first to the Admiral Benbow.

"Oh," I cried, "stop him! it's Black Dog!"

"I don't care two coppers who he is," cried Silver. "But he hasn't paid his score. Harry, run and catch him." One of the others leaped up and started in pursuit. "If he were Admiral Hawke he shall pay his score," continued Silver; and then, relinquishing my hand—"Who did you say he was? Black What?"

"Dog, sir," said I. "Has Mr. Trelawney not told you of the buccaneers? He was one of them."

"So?" cried Silver. "In my house! Ben, run and help Harry. One of those swabs, was he? Was that you drinking with him, Morgan? Step up here."

The man whom he called Morgan—an old, mahogany-faced sailor—came forward sheepishly.

"Now, Morgan," said Long John sternly, "you never clapped your eyes on that Black—Black Dog before, did you, now?"

"Not I, sir," said Morgan, with a salute.

"By the powers, Tom Morgan, it's good for you!" exclaimed the landlord. "If you had been mixed up with the like of that, you would never have put another foot in my house, you may lay to that. And what was he saying to you?"

"I don't rightly know, sir," answered Morgan.

"Do you call that a head on your shoulders, or a blessed dead-eye?" cried Long John. "Come, now, what was he jawing—v'yages, cap'ns, ships?"

"We was a-talkin' of keelhauling," answered Morgan.

"Keelhauling, was you? and a mighty suitable thing, too. Get back to your place for a lubber, Tom."

And then, as Morgan rolled back to his seat, Silver added to me in a confidential whisper, that was very flattering, as I thought: "He's an honest man, Tom Morgan, on'y stupid. And now," he ran on again aloud, "let's see—Black Dog? No, I don't know the name, not I. Yet I kind of think I've seen the swab. He used to come here with a blind beggar, he used."

"That he did, you may be sure," said I. "I knew that blind man, too. His name was Pew."

"It was!" cried Silver, now quite excited. "Pew! Ah, he looked a shark, he did! If we run down this Black Dog, now, there'll be news for Cap'n Trelawney!"

All the time he was stumping up and down the tavern on his crutch, slapping tables with his hand, and giving such a show of excitement as would have convinced an Old Bailey judge. My suspicions had been reawakened on finding Black Dog at the Spy-glass, and I watched the cook narrowly. But he was too clever for me, and by the time the two men had come back out of breath, and confessed they had lost the track in a crowd, and been scolded like thieves, I would have gone bail for the innocence of Long John Silver.

"See here, now, Hawkins," said he, "here's a blessed hard thing on a man like me, now, ain't it? There's Cap'n Trelawney—what's he to think? Here I have this confounded son of a Dutchman sitting in my own house, drinking of my own rum! Here you comes and tells me of it plain; and here I let him give us all the slip! Now, Hawkins, you do me justice with the cap'n. You're a lad, you are, but you're as smart as paint. I see that when you first came in. Now, here it is: What could I do with this old timber I hobble on? When I was an AB master mariner I'd have come up alongside of him, hand over hand, and broached him to in a brace of old shakes, I would; but now—"

And then, all of a sudden, he stopped, and his jaw dropped. "The score!" he burst out. "Three goes o' rum! Why, shiver my timbers, if I hadn't forgotten my score!"

And, falling on a bench, he laughed until the tears ran down his cheeks. I could not help joining though I did not see the joke; and we laughed together, peal after peal.

"Why, what a precious old sea calf I am!" he said at last, wiping his cheeks. "You and me should get on well, Hawkins, for I'll take my davy I should be rated ship's boy. But, come now, this won't do. Dooty is dooty, messmates. I'll put on my old cocked hat, and step along of you to Cap'n Trelawney, and report this here affair. For, mind you, it's serious, young Hawkins; and neither you nor me's come out of it with what I should make so bold as to call credit."

On our little walk along the quays he made himself the most interesting companion, telling me about the different ships that we passed by, their rig, tonnage, and nationality, explaining the work

that was going forward—how one was discharging, another taking in cargo, and a third making ready for sea; and every now and then telling me some little anecdote of ships or seamen, or repeating a nautical phrase till I had learned it perfectly. I began to see that here was one of the best of possible shipmates.

When we got to the inn, the squire and Dr. Livesey were seated together, finishing a quart of ale with a toast in it, before going aboard the schooner on a visit of inspection.

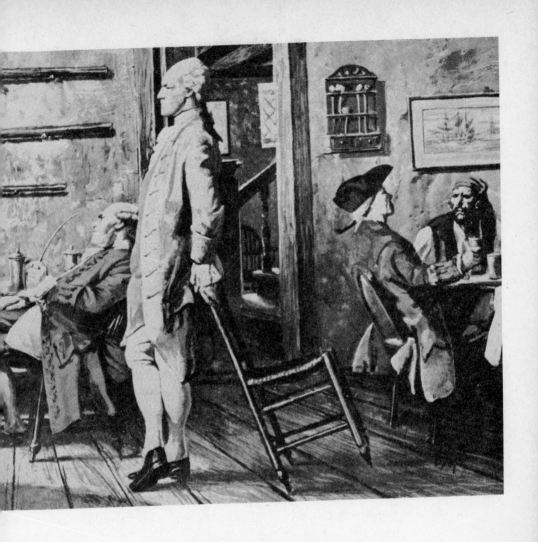

Long John told the story from first to last, with a great deal of spirit and the most perfect truth. "That was how it were, now, weren't it, Hawkins?" he would say, now and again, and I could always bear him entirely out. The two gentlemen regretted that Black Dog had got away; but we all agreed there was nothing to be done, and after he had been complimented, Long John departed.

"All hands aboard by four this afternoon," shouted the squire after him.

"Ay, ay, sir," cried the cook, in the passage.

"Well, Squire," said Dr. Livesey, "I don't put much faith in your discoveries, as a general thing; but I will say this, John Silver suits me."

"The man's a perfect trump," declared the squire.

"And now," added the doctor, "Jim may come on board with us, may he not?"

"To be sure he may," says the squire. "Take your hat, Hawkins, and we'll see the ship."

THE *HISPANIOLA* LAY some way out, and we went under the figureheads and round the sterns of many other ships, and their cables sometimes grated underneath our keel, and sometimes swung above us. At last, however, we got alongside, and were met and saluted as we stepped aboard by the mate, Mr. Arrow, a brown old sailor with earrings in his ears and a squint. He and the squire were very thick and friendly, but I soon observed that things were not the same between Mr. Trelawney and the captain, a sharp-looking man who seemed angry with everything on board.

We had hardly got down into the cabin when a sailor followed us. "Captain Smollett, sir, axing to speak with you," said he.

"I am always at the captain's orders. Show him in," said the squire.

The captain, who was close behind his messenger, entered at once, and shut the door behind him.

"Well, Captain Smollett, what have you to say? All well, I hope; all shipshape and seaworthy?"

"Well, sir," said the captain, "better speak plain, I believe, even at the risk of offense. I don't like this cruise; I don't like the men; and I don't like my officer."

"Perhaps, sir, you don't like the ship?" inquired the squire, very angry, as I could see.

"I can't speak as to that, sir, not having seen her tried," said the captain. "She seems a clever craft; more I can't say."

"Possibly, sir, you may not like your employer, either?" says the squire.

But here Dr. Livesey cut in. "Stay a bit. The captain has said too much or he has said too little, and I require an explanation of his words. You don't, you say, like this cruise?"

"I was engaged, sir, on sealed orders, to sail this ship for that gentleman where he should bid me," said the captain. "So far so good. But now I find that every man before the mast knows more than I do. I don't call that fair, now, do you?"

"No," said Dr. Livesey, "I don't."

"Next, I learn we are going after treasure—hear it from my own hands, mind you. Now, treasure is ticklish work; I don't like treasure voyages on any account; and I don't like them, above all, when they are secret, and when (begging your pardon, Mr. Trelawney) the secret has been told to the parrot."

"Silver's parrot?" asked the squire.

"It's a way of speaking. Blabbed, I mean. It's my belief neither of you gentlemen know what you are about; but I'll tell you my way of it—life or death, and a close run."

"That is all true enough," replied Dr. Livesey. "We take the risk; but we are not so ignorant as you believe us. Next, you say you don't like the crew. Are they not good seamen?"

"I don't like them, sir," returned Captain Smollett. "And I think I should have had the choosing of my own hands."

"My friend should, perhaps, have taken you along with him," replied the doctor, "but the slight was unintentional. And you don't like Mr. Arrow?"

"I don't, sir. I believe he's a good seaman; but he's too free with the crew to be a good officer."

"Well, now, captain?" asked the doctor. "What do you want?"

"Well, gentlemen, are you determined to go on this cruise?"

"Like iron," answered the squire.

"Very good," said the captain. "Then, as you've heard me very patiently, saying things that I could not prove, hear me a few words more. They are putting the powder and the arms in the forehold. Now, you have a good place under the cabin; why not put them there?—

first point. Then you are bringing four of your own people with you, and they tell me some of them are to be berthed forward. Why not give them the berths here beside the cabin?—second point."

"Any more?" asked Mr. Trelawney.

"One more. There's been too much blabbing already. I've heard myself that you have a map of an island; that there's crosses on the map to show where treasure is; and that the island lies—" And he named the latitude and longitude exactly.

"I never told that," cried the squire, "to a soul!"

"The hands know it, sir," returned the captain.

"Livesey, that must have been you or Hawkins," cried the squire.

"It doesn't much matter who it was," replied the doctor. And I could see that neither he nor the captain paid much regard to Mr. Trelawney's protestations. Neither did I, to be sure, he was so loose a talker; yet in this case I believe he was right, and that nobody had told the situation of the island.

"Well, gentlemen," said the captain, "I don't know who has this map; but I make it a point, it shall be kept secret even from me and Mr. Arrow. Otherwise I would ask you to let me resign."

"I see," said the doctor. "You wish us to keep this matter dark, and to make a garrison of the stern part of the ship, manned with my friend's own people, and provided with all the arms and powder on board. In other words, you fear a mutiny."

"Sir," said Captain Smollett, "with no intention to take offense, I deny your right to put words into my mouth. No captain would be justified in going to sea at all if he had ground enough to say that. But I am responsible for the ship's safety and the life of every man Jack aboard of her. I see things going, as I think, not quite right. And I ask you to take certain precautions, or let me resign. And that's all."

"Captain Smollett," began the doctor, with a smile, "did ever you hear the fable of the mountain and the mouse? You'll excuse me, I daresay, but you remind me of that fable. When you came in here I'll stake my wig you meant more than this."

"Doctor," said the captain, "you are smart. When I came in here

I meant to get discharged. I had no thought that Mr. Trelawney would hear a word."

"No more I would," cried the squire. "Had Livesey not been here I should have seen you to the deuce. As it is, I have heard you. I will do as you desire; but I think the worse of you."

"That's as you please, sir," said the captain. "You'll find I do my duty." And with that he took his leave.

"Trelawney," said the doctor, "I believe you have managed to get two honest men on board—that man and John Silver."

"Silver, if you like," cried the squire; "but as for that intolerable humbug, I think his conduct unmanly, unsailorly, and downright un-English."

"Well," says the doctor, "we shall see."

When we came on deck the men had begun already to take out the arms and powder, yo-ho-ing at their work, while the captain and Mr. Arrow stood by superintending.

The new arrangement was quite to my liking. The whole schooner had been overhauled; six berths had been made astern, out of the afterpart of the main hold; and this set of cabins was only joined to the galley and forecastle by a sparred passage on the port side. It had been originally meant that the captain, Mr. Arrow, Hunter, Joyce, the doctor, and the squire were to occupy the berths. Now, Redruth and I were to get two of them, and Mr. Arrow and the captain were to sleep on deck in the companion, which had been enlarged on each side till you might almost have called it a roundhouse. Very low it was still, of course; but there was room for two hammocks.

We were all hard at work changing the powder and the berths when Long John came up the side like a monkey for cleverness, and as soon as he saw what was doing, "So ho, mates!" says he, "what's this?"

"We're a-changing of the powder, Jack," answers one.

"Why, by the powers," cried Long John; "if we do, we'll miss the morning tide!"

"My orders!" said the captain, shortly. "You may go below, my man. Hands will want supper."

"Ay, ay, sir," answered the cook; and, touching his forelock, he disappeared in the direction of his galley.

"That's a good man, captain," said the doctor.

"Very likely, sir," replied Captain Smollett. "Easy with that, men—easy," he ran on to the fellows who were shifting the powder; and then suddenly observing me examining the swivel we carried amidships, a long brass nine—"Here, you ship's boy," he cried, "off with you to the cook and get some work."

And then as I was hurrying off I heard him say, quite loudly, to the doctor: "I'll have no favorites on my ship." I assure you I was quite of the squire's way of thinking, and hated the captain deeply.

V. THE VOYAGE

ALL THAT NIGHT we were in a great bustle getting things stowed in their places, and I was dog-tired when, a little before dawn, the boatswain sounded his pipe and the crew began to man the capstan bars. I might have been twice as weary, yet I would not have left the deck; all was so new and interesting to me—the brief commands, the shrill note of the whistle, the men bustling to their places in the glimmer of the ship's lanterns.

"Now, Barbecue, tip us a stave," cried one voice.

"The old one," cried another.

"Ay, ay, mates," said Long John, who was standing by, with his crutch under his arm, and at once broke out in the air and words I knew so well:

"Fifteen men on the Dead Man's Chest—"

And then the whole crew bore chorus:

"Yo-ho-ho, and a bottle of rum!"

And at the third *"ho!"* drove the bars before them with a will.

Even at that exciting moment it carried me back to the Admiral Benbow, and I seemed to hear the voice of the captain piping in the chorus. But soon the anchor was hanging dripping at the bows; soon the sails began to draw, and the *Hispaniola* had begun her voyage to the Isle of Treasure.

I am not going to relate that voyage in detail. The ship proved to be a good ship, the crew were capable seamen, and the captain thoroughly understood his business. But before we came the length of Treasure Island two or three things had happened which require to be known.

Mr. Arrow, first of all, turned out even worse than the captain had feared. He had no command among the men, and people did what they pleased with him. But that was by no means the worst of it; for after a day or two at sea he began to appear on deck with hazy eyes, stuttering tongue, and other marks of drunkenness. Time after time he was ordered below in disgrace. We could never make out where he got the drink; and when we asked him to his face, he would only laugh, if he were drunk, and if he were sober, deny solemnly that he ever tasted anything but water.

He was not only useless as an officer, but it was plain that at this rate he must soon kill himself outright; so nobody was much surprised nor very sorry when one dark night, with a head sea, he disappeared entirely and was seen no more.

"Overboard!" said the captain. "Well, gentlemen, that saves the trouble of putting him in irons."

But there we were, without a mate; and it was necessary to advance one of the men. The boatswain, Job Anderson, was the likeliest man aboard, and, though he kept his old title, he served in a way as mate. Mr. Trelawney had followed the sea, and his knowledge made him very useful, for he often took a watch himself in easy weather. And the coxswain, Israel Hands, was a careful, wily, old, experienced seaman, who could be trusted at a pinch with almost anything.

He was a great confidant of Long John Silver; and so the mention of his name leads me on to speak of our ship's cook, Barbecue, as the men called him.

Aboard ship he carried his crutch by a lanyard round his neck, to have both hands as free as possible. It was something to see him wedge the foot of the crutch against a bulkhead, and, propped against it, yielding to every movement of the ship, get on with his cooking like someone safe ashore. Still more strange was it to see him in the heaviest of weather cross the deck. He had a line or two rigged up to help him across the widest spaces—Long John's earrings, they were called; and he would hand himself from one place to another, now using the crutch, now trailing it alongside by the lanyard, as quickly as another man could walk. Yet some of the men who had sailed with him before expressed their pity to see him so reduced.

"He's no common man, Barbecue," said the coxswain to me. "He had good schooling in his young days, and can speak like a book when so minded; and brave—a lion's nothing alongside of Long John! I seen him grapple four, and knock their heads together—him unarmed."

All the crew respected and even obeyed him. To me he was unweariedly kind; and always glad to see me in the galley, which he kept as clean as a new pin; the dishes hanging up burnished, and his parrot in a cage in one corner.

"Come away, Hawkins," he would say; "come and have a yarn with John. Nobody more welcome than yourself, my son. Here's Cap'n Flint—I calls my parrot Cap'n Flint, after the famous buccaneer—here's Cap'n Flint predicting success to our v'yage. Wasn't you, Cap'n?"

And the parrot would say, with great rapidity: "Pieces of eight! pieces of eight! pieces of eight!"

"Now, that bird," John would say, "is, maybe, two hundred years old, Hawkins—they lives forever mostly; and if anybody's seen more wickedness, it must be the devil himself. She's sailed with England, the great Cap'n England, the pirate. She's been at Madagascar, and at Malabar, and Portobello. She was at the fishing up of the wrecked plate ships. It's there she learned 'Pieces of eight,' and little wonder; three hundred and fifty thousand of 'em, Hawkins!"

"Stand by to go about," the parrot would scream.

"Ah, she's a handsome craft, she is," the cook would say, and give her sugar from his pocket, and then the bird would peck at the bars

40

and swear straight on, passing belief for wickedness. "There," John would add, "you can't touch pitch and not be mucked, lad. Here's this poor old innocent bird o' mine swearing blue fire, and none the wiser, you may lay to that. She would swear the same, in a manner of speaking, before chaplain."

In the meantime, the squire and Captain Smollett were still on pretty distant terms with each other. The squire made no bones about the matter; he despised the captain. The captain, on his part, never spoke but when he was spoken to. He owned, when driven into a corner, that he seemed to have been wrong about the crew, that some of them were as brisk as he wanted to see, and all had behaved fairly well. As for the ship, he had taken a downright fancy to her. "She'll lie a point nearer the wind than a man has a right to expect of his own married wife, sir. But," he would add, "all I say is we're not home again, and I don't like the cruise."

The squire, at this, would turn away and march up and down the deck, chin in air. "A trifle more of that man," he would say, "and I should explode."

Every man on board seemed well content, and they must have been hard to please if they had been otherwise; for it is my belief there was never a ship's company so spoiled since Noah put to sea. Double grog was going on the least excuse; there was duff on odd days, as, for instance, if the squire heard it was any man's birthday, and always a barrel of apples standing broached in the waist, for anyone to help himself that had a fancy.

"Never knew good come of it yet," the captain said to Dr. Livesey. "Spoil fo'c'sle hands, make devils."

But good did come of the apple barrel, as you shall hear, for if it had not been for that, we might all have perished by the hand of treachery.

This was how it came about.

We had run up the trades to get the wind of the island we were after—I am not allowed to be more plain—and now we were running down for it with a bright lookout day and night. It was about the last day of our outward voyage; some time that night, or, at latest, before noon of the morrow, we should sight the Treasure Island. We were heading S.S.W., and had a steady breeze abeam and a quiet sea. The *Hispaniola* rolled steadily, dipping her bowsprit now and then with a whiff of spray.

Now, just after sundown, when my work was over, it occurred to me that I should like an apple. I ran on deck. The watch was all forward looking out for the island. I got bodily into the apple barrel, and found there was scarce an apple left; but sitting down there in the dark, what with the sound of the waters and rocking movement of the ship, I was on the point of falling asleep when a heavy man sat down with rather a clash close by. The barrel shook as he leaned his shoulders against it, and I was just about to jump up when the man began to speak. It was Silver's voice, and before I had heard a dozen words I would not have shown myself for all the world, but lay there, trembling and listening; for from these dozen words I understood that the lives of all the honest men aboard depended upon me alone.

VI. WHAT I HEARD IN THE APPLE BARREL

"NO, NOT I," SAID SILVER. "Flint was cap'n. I was quartermaster, along of my timber leg. The same broadside I lost my leg, old Pew lost his deadlights. It was on the *Walrus*, Flint's old ship, as I've seen a-muck with blood and fit to sink with gold."

"Ah!" cried another voice, that of the youngest hand on board, "he was the flower of the flock, was Flint!"

"I sailed with England, then with Flint," said Silver, "and now here on my own account, in a manner of speaking. I laid by nine hundred safe, from England, and two thousand after Flint. 'Tain't earning, it's saving does it, you may lay to that. Where's all England's men now? I dunno. Where's Flint's? Why, most of 'em aboard here, and glad to get the duff—been begging before that, some on 'em. Old Pew, as had lost his sight, spent twelve hundred pound in a year, like a lord in Parliament. Where is he now? Well, he's dead and under hatches; but for two year before that, shiver my timbers! the man was starving."

"Well, it ain't much use, after all," said the young seaman.

" 'Tain't much use for fools; but now, you look here: you're young, you are, but you're as smart as paint. I see that when I set my eyes on you, and I'll talk to you like a man."

You may imagine how I felt when I heard this abominable old rogue addressing another in the very same words of flattery as he had used to myself.

"Here it is about gentlemen of fortune," he ran on. "They lives rough, and they risk swinging, but they eat and drink like fighting cocks, and when a cruise is done, why it's hundreds of pounds instead of hundreds of farthings in their pockets. Now, the most goes for rum and a good fling, and to sea again in their shirts. But I puts it all away, some here, some there, and none too much anywheres, by reason of suspicion. I'm fifty, mark you; once back from this cruise I set up gentleman in earnest. And how did I begin? Before the mast, like you!"

"Well," said the other, "but all the other money's gone now, ain't it? You daren't show face in Bristol after this."

"Why, where might you suppose it was?" asked Silver, derisively.

"At Bristol, in banks and places," answered his companion.

"It were," said the cook; "it were when we weighed anchor. But my old missis has it all by now. And the Spy-glass is sold, lease and good will and rigging; and the old girl's off to meet me. I would tell you where, for I trust you, but it 'u'd make jealousy among the mates."

"And can you trust your missis?" asked the other.

"Gentlemen of fortune," returned the cook, "usually trust little among themselves. But I have a way with me, I have. There was some that was feared of Pew, and some that was feared of Flint; and Flint his own self was feared of me. They was the roughest crew afloat, was Flint's. I tell you, I'm not a boasting man, but when I was quarter-master, lambs wasn't the word for Flint's old buccaneers. Ah, you may be sure of yourself in old John's ship."

"Well, I tell you now," replied the lad, "I didn't half a quarter like the job till I had this talk with you; but here's my hand on it now."

"And a brave lad you were, and smart, too," answered Silver, shaking hands so heartily that the barrel shook, "and a finer figurehead for a gentleman of fortune I never clapped eyes on."

By this time I had begun to understand the meaning of their terms. By a "gentleman of fortune" they meant neither more nor less than a common pirate, and the scene I had overheard was the last act in the corruption of one of the honest hands—perhaps the last one left aboard. But on this point I was soon to be relieved, for, Silver giving a little whistle, a third man strolled up and sat down by the party.

"Dick's square," said Silver.

"Oh, I know'd Dick was square," returned the voice of Israel Hands. "He's no fool, is Dick. But look here, Barbecue, how long are we a-going to stand off and on like a blessed bumboat? I've had a'most enough of Cap'n Smollett! I want to go into that cabin, I do. I want their pickles and wines, and that."

"Israel," said Silver, "your head ain't much account. But you're able to hear, I reckon. Now, here's what I say: you'll berth forward, and you'll live hard, and you'll speak soft, and you'll keep sober, till I give the word."

"Well, I don't say no, do I?" growled the coxswain. "What I say is, when? That's what I say."

"When!" cried Silver. "The last moment I can manage; and that's when. Here's a first-rate seaman, Cap'n Smollett, sails the blessed ship for us. Here's this squire and doctor with a map and such—I don't know where it is, do I? No more do you, says you. Well, then, I mean this squire and doctor shall find the stuff, and help us to get it aboard. Then we'll see. If I was sure of you all, sons of double Dutchmen, I'd have Cap'n Smollett navigate us halfway back again before I struck; then we'd have no blessed miscalculations and a spoonful of water a day. But I know the sort you are. I'll finish with 'em at the island, as soon's the blunt's on board, and a pity it is. But you're never happy till you're drunk. Slit my sides, I've a sick heart to sail with the likes of you!"

"Easy all, Long John," cried Israel. "Who's a-crossin' of you?"

"Why, how many tall ships, think ye, have I seen lain aboard, and how many brisk lads drying in the sun at Execution Dock?" cried Silver. "And all for this same hurry and hurry and hurry. If you would on'y lay your course, and p'int to windward, you would ride in carriages, you would. But you'll have your mouthful of rum tomorrow, and go hang. Pew was that sort, and died a beggarman. Flint was, and he died of rum. Ah, they was a sweet crew, they was! on'y where are they?"

"But," asked Dick, "when we do lay 'em athwart, what are we to do with 'em, anyhow?"

"There's a man for me!" cried the cook, admiringly. "That's what I call business. Well, what would you think? Put 'em ashore like maroons? That would have been England's way. Or cut 'em down like that much pork? That would have been Flint's or Billy Bones's."

"Billy was the man for that," said Israel. "'Dead men don't bite,' says he."

"Right you are," said Silver. "Mark you here: I'm an easy man, but this time it's serious. Dooty is dooty, mates. I give my vote—death. When I'm in Parlyment, and riding in my coach, I don't want none of these sea lawyers in the cabin a-coming home, unlooked for, like the devil at prayers. Wait is what I say; but when the time comes, why, let her rip!"

"John," cries the coxswain, "you're a man!"

"You'll say so, Israel, when you see," said Silver. "Only one thing I claim—I claim Trelawney. I'll wring his calf's head off his body with these hands. Dick!" he added, breaking off, "you just jump up, like a sweet lad, and get me an apple to wet my pipe like."

You may fancy the terror I was in! I heard Dick begin to rise, and then the voice of Hands exclaimed: "Oh, stow that! Let's have a go of the rum."

"Dick," said Silver, "I trust you. I've a gauge on the keg, mind. There's the key; fill a pannikin and bring it up."

Terrified as I was, I could not help thinking to myself that this must have been how Mr. Arrow got the strong waters that had destroyed him.

Dick was gone but a little while, and during his absence Israel spoke straight on in the cook's ear. It was but a word or two that I could catch, and yet I gathered some important news; for this whole clause was audible: "Not another man of them'll jine." Hence there were still faithful men on board.

When Dick returned, one after another of the trio took the pannikin and drank—one "To luck"; another with a "Here's to old Flint"; and Silver himself saying, in a kind of song, "Here's to ourselves, and hold your luff, plenty of prizes and plenty of duff."

Just then a sort of brightness fell upon me in the barrel, and, looking up, I found the moon had risen and was shining white on the luff of the foresail; and almost at the same time the voice of the lookout shouted, "Land ho!"

I COULD HEAR PEOPLE tumbling up from the cabin and the fo'c'sle; and, slipping outside my barrel, I dived behind the foresail, made a double toward the stern, and came out upon the open deck in time to join Hunter and Dr. Livesey in the rush for the weather bow. There all hands were already congregated. A belt of fog had lifted with the appearance of the moon. Away to the southwest we saw two low hills, and rising behind one of them a third and higher hill, whose peak was still buried in the fog.

So much I saw, almost in a dream, for I had not yet recovered from my horrid fear of a minute or two before. Then I heard the voice of Captain Smollett issuing orders for a course change.

"And now, men," said the captain, when all was sheeted home, "has any of you ever seen that land ahead?"

"I have, sir," said Silver. "I've watered there with a trader I was cook in."

"The anchorage is on the south, behind an islet, I fancy?"

"Yes, sir; Skeleton Island they calls it. It were a main place for pirates once, and a hand we had on board knowed all their names for it. That hill to the nor'ard they calls the Foremast Hill; there are three hills in a row running south'ard—fore, main, and mizzen, sir. But the main—that's the big un with the cloud on it—they usually calls the Spy-glass, by reason of a lookout they kept when they was in the anchorage cleaning; for it's there they cleaned their ships, sir, asking your pardon."

"I have a chart here," says Captain Smollett. "See if that's the place."

Long John's eyes burned in his head as he took the chart; but by the fresh look of the paper, I knew he was doomed to disappointment. This was not the map we found in Billy Bones's chest, but a copy, complete in all things with the single exception of the red crosses and the written notes. Sharp as must have been this annoyance, Silver had the strength of mind to hide it.

"Yes, sir," said he, "this is the spot, and very prettily drawed out. Ay, here it is: Captain Kidd's Anchorage—just the name my shipmate called it. There's a strong current runs along the south, and then away nor'ard up the west coast. Right you was, sir, to haul your wind and keep the weather of the island."

"Thank you, my man," says Captain Smollett. "I'll ask you, later on, to give us a help. You may go."

I was surprised at the coolness with which John avowed his knowledge of the island; and I own I was half frightened when I saw him drawing nearer to myself. I had, by this time, taken such a horror of his cruelty, duplicity, and power, that I could scarce conceal a shudder when he laid his hand upon my arm.

"Ah," says he, "this is a sweet spot, this island—a sweet spot for a lad to get ashore on. You'll bathe, and you'll climb trees, and you'll hunt goats, you will. When you want to go a bit of exploring, you just ask old John, and he'll put up a snack for you to take along." And clapping me in the friendliest way upon the shoulder, he hobbled off.

Captain Smollett, the squire, and Dr. Livesey were talking together on the quarterdeck, and, anxious as I was to tell them my story, I durst not interrupt them openly. While I was still casting about in my thoughts to find some probable excuse, Dr. Livesey called me to his side. He had left his pipe below, and had meant that I should fetch it; but as soon as I was near enough not to be overheard, I broke out immediately: "Doctor, let me speak. Get the captain and squire down to the cabin, and then make some pretense to send for me. I have terrible news."

The doctor changed countenance a little, but next moment he was master of himself. "Thank you, Jim," said he, quite loudly, "that was all I wanted to know," as if he had asked me a question.

And with that he rejoined the other two. They spoke together for a little, and though none of them started, or raised his voice, it was plain that Dr. Livesey had communicated my request; for the next thing I heard was the captain giving an order to Job Anderson, and all hands were piped on deck.

"My lads," said Captain Smollett, "this land that we have sighted is the place we have been sailing to. Mr. Trelawney, being a very openhanded gentleman, has just asked me a word or two, and as I was able to tell him that every man on board had done his duty alow and aloft, why, he and I and the doctor are going below to the cabin to drink *your* health and luck, and you'll have grog served out for you to drink *our* health and luck. I think it handsome. And if you think as I do, you'll give a good sea cheer for the gentleman that does it."

The cheer that followed rang out so full and hearty, that I could hardly believe these same men were plotting for our blood.

"One more cheer for Cap'n Smollett," cried Long John, when the first had subsided. And this also was given with a will.

On the top of that the three gentlemen went below, and not long after word was sent forward that I was wanted in the cabin. I found them seated round the table, a bottle of Spanish wine and some raisins before them, and the doctor smoking away, with his wig on his lap, and that, I knew, was a sign that he was agitated.

"Now, Hawkins," said the squire, "speak up."

As short as I could make it, I told the whole details of Silver's conversation. Nobody interrupted me till I was done, but the three of them kept their eyes upon my face from first to last. Then they made me sit down at the table beside them, poured me out a glass of wine and, one after the other, drank my good health, and their service to me, for my luck and courage.

"Now, Captain," said the squire, "you were right, and I was wrong. I own myself an ass, and I await your orders."

"No more an ass than I, sir," returned the captain. "I never heard of a crew that meant mutiny but what showed signs before, for any man that had an eye in his head to see the mischief and take steps according. But this crew," he added, "beats me."

"Captain," said the doctor, "with your permission, that's Silver. A very remarkable man."

"He'd look remarkably well from a yardarm, sir," returned the captain. "But this is talk; this don't lead to anything. I see three or four points, and with Mr. Trelawney's permission I'll name them."

"You, sir, are the captain. It is for you to speak," says Mr. Trelawney, grandly.

"First point," began Mr. Smollett. "We must go on, because we can't turn back. If I gave the word to go about they would rise at once. Second point, we have time before us—at least until this treasure's found. Third point, there are faithful hands. Now, sir, it's got to come to blows sooner or later; and what I propose is, to take time by the forelock, as the saying is, and come to blows some fine day when they least expect it. We can count, I take it, on your own home servants, Mr. Trelawney?"

"As upon myself," declared the squire.

"Three," reckoned the captain, "ourselves make seven, counting Hawkins here. Now, about the honest hands?"

"Most likely Trelawney's own men," said the doctor; "those he had picked up for himself before he lit on Silver."

"Nay," replied the squire, "Hands was one of mine."

"I did think I could trust Hands," added the captain.

"And to think that they're all Englishmen!" broke out the squire.

"Well, gentlemen," said the captain, "we must lay to, and keep a bright lookout. It would be pleasanter to come to blows. But there's no help for it till we know our men."

"Jim, here," said the doctor, "can help us more than anyone. The men are not shy with him, and Jim is a noticing lad."

"Hawkins, I put prodigious faith in you," added the squire.

I began to feel pretty desperate at this, for I felt altogether helpless; and yet, by an odd train of circumstances, it was indeed through me that safety came. In the meantime, talk as we pleased, there were only seven out of the twenty-six on whom we knew we could rely; and out of these seven one was a boy, so that the grown men on our side were six to their nineteen.

VII. HOW MY SHORE ADVENTURE BEGAN

THE APPEARANCE OF THE ISLAND when I came on deck next morning was altogether changed. We had made a great deal of way during the night, and were now lying becalmed about half a mile to the southeast of the low eastern coast. Gray-colored woods covered a large part of the surface. This even tint was broken up by streaks of yellow sandbank in the lower lands, and by many tall trees of the pine family, outtopping the others; but the general coloring was uniform and sad. The hills ran up clear above the vegetation in spires of naked rock. All were strangely shaped, and the Spy-glass, the tallest on the island, was likewise the strangest in configuration; running up sheer from almost every side, and cut off at the top like a pedestal to put a statue on.

The *Hispaniola* was rolling scuppers under in the ocean swell. The booms were tearing at the blocks, the rudder was banging to and fro, and the whole ship creaked. I had to cling tight to the backstay, the world turning giddily before my eyes. Perhaps it was this—perhaps it was the look of the island with its gray, melancholy woods and wild stone spires—at any rate, although the sun shone bright and hot, my heart sank, as the saying is, into my boots; and from that first look onward I hated the very thought of Treasure Island.

We had a dreary morning's work before us, for there was no sign of any wind, and the boats had to be got out and manned, and the ship warped three or four miles round the corner of the island and up the narrow passage to the haven behind Skeleton Island. I volunteered for one of the boats, where I had, of course, no business. The heat was sweltering, and the men grumbled over their work. Anderson was in command of my boat, and instead of keeping the crew in order he grumbled as loud as the worst.

"Well," he said, with an oath, "it's not forever."

I thought this a very bad sign; for, up to that day, the men had gone briskly about their business; but the very sight of the island had relaxed the cords of discipline.

All the way in Long John stood by the steersman and conned the ship. He knew the passage like the palm of his hand, and he never hesitated once.

We brought up just where the anchor was in the chart, about a third of a mile from either shore, the mainland on one side and Skeleton Island on the other. The bottom was clean sand. The plunge of our anchor sent up clouds of birds wheeling and crying over the woods; but in less than a minute they were down again, and all was once more silent.

The place was entirely landlocked, buried in woods, the trees coming right down to high-water mark. Two little rivers, or, rather, two swamps, emptied into this pond, as you might call it; and the foliage round that part of the shore had a kind of poisonous brightness. A peculiar stagnant smell hung over the anchorage—a smell of sodden leaves and rotting tree trunks. I observed the doctor sniffing, like someone tasting a bad egg. "I don't know about treasure," he said, "but I'll stake my wig there's fever here."

If the conduct of the men had been alarming in the boat, it became truly threatening when they had come back aboard. The slightest order was received with a black look, and grudgingly and carelessly obeyed. Mutiny, it was plain, hung over us like a thundercloud. And it was not only we of the cabin party who perceived the danger. Long John went from group to group, spending himself in good advice. He fairly outstripped himself in willingness and civility; he was all smiles to everyone. If an order were given John would be on his crutch in an instant with a cheery "Ay, ay, sir!" And when there was nothing else to do he kept up one long song after another, as if to conceal the discontent of the rest.

Of all the gloomy features of that gloomy afternoon, this obvious anxiety on the part of Long John appeared the worst.

We held a council in the cabin.

"Sir," said the captain, "if I risk another order the whole ship'll come about our ears. You see, sir, here it is. I get a rough answer, do I not? If I speak back, pikes will be going in two shakes; if I don't, Silver will see there's something under that, and the game's up. Now, we've only one man to rely on."

"And who is that?" asked the squire.

"Silver, sir. He's as anxious as you and I to smother things up. Let's allow the men an afternoon ashore. If they all go, why, we'll fight the ship. If they none of them go, we hold the cabin, and God defend the right. If some go, you mark my words, sir, Silver'll bring 'em aboard again as mild as lambs."

It was so decided; loaded pistols were served out to all the sure men: Hunter, Joyce, and Redruth were taken into our confidence, and then the captain went on deck and addressed the crew. "My lads," said he, "we've had a hot day, and are all tired. The boats are still in the water; and as many as please can go ashore for the afternoon. I'll fire a gun half an hour before sundown."

I believe the silly fellows must have thought they would break their shins over treasure as soon as they were landed; for they all came out of their sulks in a moment and gave a cheer that started the echo in a faraway hill.

The captain then whipped out of sight, leaving Silver to arrange the party, and I fancy it was as well he did so. Had he been on deck, he could no longer have pretended not to understand the situation. It was as plain as day. Silver was the captain, and a mighty rebellious crew he had of it. At last, however, the party was made up. Six fellows were to stay on board, and the remaining thirteen, including Silver, began to embark.

Then it was that there came into my head the first of the mad notions that contributed so much to save our lives. If six men were left by Silver, it was plain our party could not take and fight the ship; and since only six were left, it was equally plain that the cabin party had no present need of my assistance. It occurred to me at once to go ashore. In a jiffy I had slipped over the side and curled up in the fore-sheets of the nearest boat, and almost at the same moment she shoved off.

No one took notice of me, only the bow oar saying: "Is that you, Jim? Keep your head down." But Silver, from the other boat, looked sharply over and called out to know if that were me; and from that moment I began to regret what I had done.

The crews raced for the beach; but the boat I was in shot ahead of her consort, and the bow had struck among the shoreside trees, and I had caught a branch and swung myself out, and plunged into the nearest thicket, while Silver and the rest were still a hundred yards behind. "Jim, Jim!" I heard him shouting.

But I paid no heed; jumping, ducking, and breaking through, I ran straight before my nose, till I could run no longer.

I WAS SO PLEASED at having given the slip to Long John that I began to enjoy myself and look around me. I had crossed a marshy tract full of willows, bulrushes, and odd, swampy trees; and I had now come out upon an open piece of undulating, sandy country dotted with a great number of contorted trees not unlike oaks, but pale in the foliage, like willows. Going on I came to a long thicket of these oaklike trees—live oaks, I heard afterward they should be called—which grew low along the sand like brambles. The thicket stretched down to the margin of the broad, reedy fen, through which the nearest of the little rivers soaked its way to the anchorage.

All at once a wild duck flew up with a quack from among the bulrushes; and soon over the whole marsh a great cloud of birds hung screaming and circling in the air. I judged at once that some of my shipmates must be drawing near along the borders of the fen. Nor was I deceived; for soon I heard the distant tones of a human voice, which grew steadily louder and nearer. This put me in a great fear, and I crawled under cover of the nearest live oak and squatted there, harkening, as silent as a mouse.

Another voice answered; and then the first voice, which I now recognized to be Silver's, ran on for a long while. At last the speakers seemed to have paused, and perhaps to have sat down; for not only did they cease to draw any nearer, but the birds began to settle again to their places in the swamp.

And now I began to feel that since I had been so foolhardy as to come ashore with these desperadoes, the least I could do was to draw as close as I could manage, and overhear them at their councils. Crawling on all fours, I made slowly toward the speakers; till at last, raising my head to an aperture among the leaves, I could see down into a little green dell beside the marsh, where Long John and another of the crew stood face to face.

The sun beat full upon them. Silver had thrown his hat beside him on the ground, and his great smooth, blond face, all shining with heat, was lifted to the other man's in a kind of appeal. "Tom," he was saying, "it's because I thinks gold dust of you—gold dust! If I hadn't took to you like pitch, do you think I'd have been here a-warning of you? All's up—you can't make nor mend; it's to save your neck that I'm a-speaking, and if one of the wild uns knew it, where 'u'd I be?"

"Silver," said the other man—and his voice shook like a taut rope—"Silver," says he, "you're old, and you're honest, or has the name for it; and you've money, too; and you're brave, or I'm mistook. And will you tell me you'll let yourself be led away with that kind of a mess of swabs? Not you! As sure as God sees me, I'd sooner lose my hand. If I turn agin my dooty—"

And then all of a sudden he was interrupted by a noise. I had found one of the honest hands—well, here came news of another. Faraway out in the marsh there arose cries of anger, then one horrid, long-drawn scream.

Tom leaped at the sound; but Silver did not wink an eye. He stood where he was, resting lightly on his crutch, watching his companion like a snake about to spring.

"John!" said the sailor, stretching out his hand.

"Hands off!" cried Silver, leaping back.

"Hands off, if you like, John Silver," said the other. "It's a black conscience that can make you feared of me. But, in Heaven's name, tell me what was that?"

"That?" returned Silver, smiling away, but warier than ever. "That? Oh, I reckon that'll be Alan."

And at this poor Tom flashed out like a hero. "Alan!" he cried. "Then rest his soul for a true seaman! And as for you, John Silver, long you've been a mate of mine, but you're mate of mine no more. If I die like a dog, I'll die in my dooty. You've killed Alan. Kill me, too, if you can. But I defies you."

And with that this brave fellow turned his back on the cook, and set off walking for the beach. But he was not destined to go far. With a cry John seized the branch of a tree, whipped the crutch out of his armpit, and sent that uncouth missile hurtling through the air. It struck poor Tom, point foremost, and with stunning violence, right between the shoulders in the middle of his back. His hands flew up, he gave a sort of gasp, and fell.

Silver, agile as a monkey, even without leg or crutch, was on the top of him next moment, and had twice buried his knife up to the hilt in that defenseless body.

I do not know what it rightly is to faint, but I do know that for the next little while the whole world swam away before me in a whirling mist; Silver and the birds and the tall Spy-glass hilltop going round and round before my eyes, and all manner of bells ringing and distant voices shouting in my ears.

When I came again to myself the monster had his crutch under his arm, his hat upon his head. Just before him Tom lay motionless upon the sward; but the murderer minded him not a whit, cleansing his bloodstained knife the while upon a wisp of grass. Now he put his hand into his pocket, brought out a whistle, and blew a blast upon it. The signal instantly awoke my fears. More men would be coming. I might be discovered. They had already slain Tom and Alan. Might not I come next?

I began to crawl back to the more open portion of the wood. As I did so I could hear hails coming and going between the old buccaneer and his comrades, and this sound of danger lent me wings. As soon as I was clear of the thicket I ran as I never ran before, and as I ran fear grew upon me until it turned into a kind of frenzy. Indeed, could anyone be more entirely lost than I? When the gun fired, how should I dare to go down to the boats among those fiends? Would not the first who saw me wring my neck like a snipe's? Would not my absence itself be an evidence to them of my alarm, and therefore of my fatal knowledge? It was all over, I thought. Good-by to the *Hispaniola;* good-by to the squire, the doctor, the captain!

All this while I was still running, and I had drawn near to the foot of the little hill with the two peaks, and had got into a part of the island where the live oaks grew more widely apart. Mingled with these were a few scattered pines, some fifty, some nearer seventy, feet high. The air, too, smelled more freshly than down beside the marsh.

And here a fresh alarm brought me to a standstill with a thumping heart.

From the side of the hill a spout of gravel was dislodged and fell rattling through the trees. My eyes turned instinctively in that direction, and I saw a figure leap behind the trunk of a pine. What it was, whether bear or man or monkey, I could in no wise tell. But the terror of this new apparition brought me to a stand.

I was now, it seemed, cut off upon both sides; behind me the murderers, before me this lurking nondescript. And immediately I began to prefer the dangers I knew to those I knew not. I turned on my heel and, looking over my shoulder, began to retrace my steps in the direction of the boats. Instantly the figure reappeared, and, making a wide circuit, began to head me off. From trunk to trunk it flitted like a deer, running manlike on two legs, but unlike any man I had ever seen, stooping almost double as it ran. Yet a man it was; I could no longer be in doubt about that.

The mere fact that he was a man, however wild, had somewhat reassured me, and my fear of Silver began to revive in proportion. The recollection of my pistol flashed into my mind and, as soon as I remembered I was not defenseless, I set my face resolutely for this man of the island and walked briskly toward him.

He was concealed by this time behind another tree trunk; but as soon as I began to move in his direction he reappeared and took a step to meet me. Then he drew back, came forward again, and at last, to my wonder and confusion, threw himself on his knees and held out his clasped hands in supplication.

"Who are you?" I asked.

"Ben Gunn," he answered, and his voice sounded like a rusty lock. "I'm poor Ben Gunn, I am; and I haven't spoke with a Christian these three years."

I could now see that he was a white man like myself. His skin was burnt by the sun; and his fair eyes looked startling in so dark a face. He was clothed with tatters of old ship's canvas and old sea cloth; and this extraordinary patchwork was all held together by a system of the most incongruous fastenings—brass buttons, bits of stick, and loops of tarry gaskin. About his waist he wore an old brass-buckled leather belt.

"Three years!" I cried. "Were you shipwrecked?"

"Nay, mate," said he— "marooned."

I had heard the word, and I knew it stood for a horrible kind of punishment common among the buccaneers, in which the offender is put ashore on some desolate and distant island and left behind.

"Marooned three years agone," he continued, "and lived on goats since then, and berries, and oysters. But, mate, my heart is sore for Christian diet. You mightn't have a piece of cheese about you, now?

No? Well, many's the long night I've dreamed of cheese—toasted, mostly—and woke up again, and here I were."

"If ever I can get on board again," said I, "you shall have cheese by the stone."

All this time he had been feeling the stuff of my jacket, looking at my boots, and generally showing a childish pleasure in the presence of a fellow creature. But at my last words he perked up into a kind of startled shyness. "If ever you can get on board again, says you? Why, now, who's to hinder you?"

"Not you, I know," was my reply.

"And right you was," he cried. "Now you—what do you call yourself, mate?"

"Jim," I told him.

"Jim, Jim," says he, quite pleased apparently. "Well, now, Jim, I've lived that rough as you'd be ashamed to hear of. Now, you wouldn't think I had had a pious mother—to look at me?"

"Why, no, not in particular," I answered.

"Ah, well," said he, "but I had—remarkable pious. And I was a civil, pious boy, and could rattle off my catechism that fast as you couldn't tell one word from another. And, Jim"—looking all round him and lowering his voice to a whisper—"I'm rich."

I now felt sure that the poor fellow had gone crazy in his solitude, and I suppose I must have shown the feeling in my face, for he repeated the statement hotly: "Rich, rich! I says. And I'll make a man of you, Jim. Ah, Jim, you'll bless your stars, you will, you was the first that found me!" And at this there came a shadow over his face, and he tightened his grasp upon my hand. "Now, Jim, you tell me true; that ain't Flint's ship?" he asked.

At this I had a happy inspiration. I began to believe that I had found an ally, and I answered him at once. "It's not Flint's ship, and Flint is dead; but there are some of Flint's hands aboard; worse luck for the rest of us."

"Not a man with one leg?" he gasped.

"Silver?" I asked.

The captain had risen earlier than usual, and set out down the beach, his

cutlass swinging under the old blue coat, his brass telescope under his arm.

As the blow still hung impending, I leaped in a trice upon one side, and,

missing my foot in the soft sand, rolled headlong down the slope.

Right before us we saw the wreck of a ship in the last stages of dilapidation.

At the foot of a pretty big pine, and involved in a green creeper, a human skeleton lay, with a few shreads of clothing, on the ground.

"Ah, Silver!" says he; "that were his name."

"He's the cook; and the ringleader, too."

He was still holding me by the wrist, and at that he gave it quite a wring. "If you was sent by Long John," he said, "I'm as good as pork, and I know it."

I had made up my mind in a moment, and told him the whole story of our voyage, and the predicament in which we found ourselves. He heard me with the keenest interest, and when I had done he patted me on the head. "You're a good lad, Jim," he said, "and you're all in a clove hitch, ain't you? Well, you just put your trust in Ben Gunn. Would you think it likely, now, that your squire would prove a liberal-minded one in case of help?"

I told him the squire was the most liberal of men.

"Ay, but you see, I didn't mean giving me a gate to keep, and a suit of livery clothes, Jim. What I mean is, would he be likely to come down to the toon of, say, one thousand pounds out of the money that's as good as a man's own already?"

"I am sure he would," said I. "As it was, all hands were to share."

"*And* a passage home?" he added, with a look of great shrewdness.

"Why," I cried, "the squire's a gentleman. And besides, if we got rid of the others, we should want you to help work the vessel home."

"Ah," said he, "so you would." And he seemed very much relieved. "Now, I'll tell you what," he went on. "So much I'll tell you, and no more. I were in Flint's ship when he buried the treasure; he and six along—six strong seamen. They were ashore nigh on a week, and us standing off and on in the old *Walrus*. One fine day up went the signal, and here come Flint by himself in a little boat, and his head done up in a blue scarf. Mortal white he looked; but, there he was, you mind, and the six all dead—dead and buried. How he done it not a man aboard us could make out. It was him against six. Billy Bones was the mate; Long John, he was quartermaster; and they asked him where the treasure was. 'Ah,' says he, 'you can go ashore, if you like, and stay,' he says; 'but as for the ship, she'll beat up for more, by thunder!'

"Well, I was in another ship three years back, and we sighted this

island. 'Boys,' said I, 'here's Flint's treasure; let's land and find it.'
The cap'n was displeased at that; but my messmates were all of a
mind, and landed. Twelve days they looked for it, and every day they
had the worse word for me, until one fine morning all hands went
aboard. 'As for you, Benjamin Gunn,' says they, 'here's a musket,'
they says, 'and a spade and pickax. You can stay here and find Flint's
money for yourself.'

"Well, Jim, three years have I been here, and not a bite of Christian
diet from that day to this. But now, you look here. Do I look like a
man before the mast? No, says you. Nor I weren't, neither, I says."

With that he winked and pinched me hard. "Just you mention them
words to your squire," he went on. "Nor he weren't, neither—that's
the words. Three years he were the man of this island, light and dark,
fair and rain; and sometimes he would, maybe, think upon a prayer
(says you), and sometimes he would, maybe, think of his old mother,
so be as she's alive (you'll say); but the most part of Gunn's time
(this is what you'll say)—the most part of his time was took up with
another matter. And then you'll give him a nip, like I do." And he
pinched me again in the most confidential manner.

"Then," he continued—"then you'll say: Gunn is a good man
(you'll say), and he puts a precious sight more confidence—a precious
sight, mind that—in a gen'leman born than in these gen'lemen of
fortune, having been one hisself."

"Well," I said, "I don't understand one word that you've been saying. But that's neither here nor there; for how am I to get on board?"

"Well, there's my boat, that I made with my two hands. I keep her
under the white rock. If the worst comes to the worst, we might try
that after dark. Hi!" he broke out, "what's that?"

For just then, although the sun had still an hour or two to run,
all the echoes of the island bellowed to the thunder of a cannon.

"They have begun to fight!" I cried. "Follow me." And I began to
run toward the anchorage, my terrors all forgotten; while, close at my
side, the marooned man trotted easily and lightly.

"Left, left," says he; "keep to your left hand, mate Jim! Under the trees with you! Theer's where I killed my first goat. They don't come down here now. Ah! and there's the cetemery"—cemetery, he must have meant. "You see the mounds? I come here and prayed, nows and thens, when I thought maybe Sunday would be about doo." So he kept talking as I ran, neither expecting nor receiving any answer.

The cannon shot was followed, after a considerable interval, by a volley of small arms. Another pause, and then, not a quarter of a mile in front of me, I beheld the Union Jack flutter in the air above a wood.

VIII. NARRATIVE CONTINUED BY THE DOCTOR: HOW THE SHIP WAS ABANDONED

IT WAS ABOUT half past one—three bells in the sea phrase—that the two boats went ashore from the *Hispaniola*. The captain, the squire, and I were talking matters over in the cabin. Had there been a breath of wind we should have fallen on the six mutineers who were left aboard with us, slipped our cable, and away to sea. But the wind was wanting; and, to complete our helplessness, down came Hunter with the news that Jim Hawkins had slipped into a boat and was gone ashore with the rest.

It never occurred to us to doubt Jim Hawkins; but we were alarmed for his safety. We ran on deck. The pitch was bubbling in the seams; the nasty stench of the place turned me sick; if ever man smelled fever and dysentery, it was in that abominable anchorage. The six scoundrels were sitting grumbling under a sail in the forecastle; ashore we could see the gigs made fast, and a man sitting in each, hard by where the river runs in. One of them was whistling "Lillibullero."

Waiting was a strain; and it was decided that Hunter and I should go ashore with the jolly boat in quest of information. The gigs had leaned to their left; but Hunter and I pulled straight in, in the direction of the stockade upon the chart. The two who were left guarding their boats seemed in a bustle at our appearance; "Lillibullero" stopped off, and I could see the pair discussing what they ought to do. Had they gone and told Silver, all might have turned out differently;

but they had their orders, I suppose, and decided to sit quietly where they were and hark back again to "Lillibullero."

There was a slight bend in the coast, and I steered so as to put it between us; even before we landed we had thus lost sight of the gigs. I jumped out and came as near running as I durst, with a brace of pistols ready primed for safety. I had not gone a hundred yards when I came on the stockade.

This was how it was: a spring of clear water rose almost at the top of a knoll. Well, on the knoll, and enclosing the spring, they had clapped a stout log house, fit to hold two score people, and loopholed for musketry on every side. All round this they had cleared a wide space, and then there was a paling six feet high, too strong to pull down without time and labor, and too open to shelter the besiegers. The people in the log house, short of a complete surprise, might have held the place against a regiment.

What particularly took my fancy was the spring. For, though we had in the *Hispaniola* plenty of arms and ammunition, and things to eat, and excellent wines, there had been one thing overlooked—we had no water. I was thinking this over when there came ringing over the island the cry of a man at the point of death. I was not new to violent death—I have served his Royal Highness the Duke of Cumberland, and got a wound myself at Fontenoy—but I know my pulse went dot and carry one. Jim Hawkins is gone, I thought.

With no time lost I returned to the jolly boat. Hunter pulled a good oar. We made the water fly; and I was soon aboard the schooner. I found them all shaken, as was natural. The squire was sitting down, as white as a sheet, thinking of the harm he had led us to, the good soul! and one of the six forecastle hands was little better.

"There's a man," says Captain Smollett, nodding toward him, "new to this work. He came nigh fainting when he heard the cry. Another touch of the rudder and that man would join us."

I told my plan to the captain, and between us we settled on the details of its accomplishment. We put old Redruth in the gallery between the cabin and the forecastle, with three or four loaded muskets and a mattress for protection. Hunter brought the boat round under the stern port, and Joyce and I set to work loading her with powder tins, muskets, bags of biscuits, kegs of pork, a cask of cognac, and my invaluable medicine chest.

In the meantime the squire and the captain stayed on deck, and the latter hailed the coxswain, who was the principal man aboard. "Mr. Hands," he said, "here are two of us with a brace of pistols each. If any of you make a signal, that man's dead."

They were quite taken aback, and, after a consultation, all tumbled down the fore companion, thinking, no doubt, to take us on the rear. But when they saw Redruth waiting for them in the sparred gallery they went about at once, and a head popped out on deck.

"Down, dog!" cries the captain. And the head popped back again, and we heard no more for a time of these fainthearted seamen.

By this time we had the jolly boat loaded as much as we dared. Joyce and I got out through the stern port, and we made for shore again. This second trip fairly aroused the watchers along the shore. "Lillibullero" was dropped again; and before we lost sight of them behind the little point one of them disappeared inland. I had half a mind to change my plan and destroy their boats, but I feared that Silver and the others might be close at hand and all might be lost by trying for too much.

We had soon touched land in the same place as before, and set to provision the blockhouse. All three made the first journey, heavily laden, and tossed our stores over the palisade. Then, leaving Joyce to guard them—one man, to be sure, but with half a dozen muskets— Hunter and I returned to the jolly boat and loaded ourselves once more. So we proceeded till the cargo was bestowed, when the two servants took up their position in the blockhouse, and I, with all my power, sculled back to the *Hispaniola*.

That we should have risked a second boatload seems more daring than it really was. Not one of the men ashore had a musket, and before they could get within range of pistol shooting we flattered ourselves we should be able to account for half a dozen at least.

The squire was waiting for me at the stern window. He caught the painter and made it fast, and we fell to loading the boat for our very lives. Pork, powder, and biscuit was the cargo, with only a musket and a cutlass apiece for the squire and me and Redruth and the captain. The rest of the arms and powder we dropped overboard.

By this time the tide was beginning to ebb, and the ship was swinging round to her anchor. Voices were heard faintly hallooing in the direction of the two gigs; and though this reassured us for Joyce and Hunter, who were well to the eastward, it warned our party to be off. Redruth retreated from the gallery, and dropped into the boat, which we then brought round to the ship's counter to be handier for Captain Smollett.

"Now, men," said he, "do you hear me?" There was no answer. "Abraham Gray, it's to you I am speaking." Still no reply. "I am leaving this ship, and I order you to follow your captain. I have my watch here in my hand; I give you thirty seconds to join me in." Still no reply.

"Come, my fine fellow," continued the captain. "I'm risking my life and the lives of these good gentlemen every second."

There was a sudden scuffle, a sound of blows, and out burst Abraham Gray with a knife cut on his cheek.

"I'm with you, sir," said he.

And the next moment he and the captain had dropped aboard of us, and we shoved off.

This trip was quite different from any of the others. In the first place, the little boat was gravely overloaded. Five grown men, and three of them—Trelawney, Redruth, and the captain—over six feet high, were already more than she was meant to carry. Add to that the powder, pork, and bread bags. Several times we shipped a little water, and my breeches were soaking wet before we had gone a hundred yards.

In the second place, the ebb was now making. Even the ripples were a danger to our overloaded craft; but the worst of it was that the current was sweeping us westward, away from our proper landing place behind the point.

"I cannot keep her head for the stockade, sir," said I to the captain.

I was steering, while he and Redruth were at the oars. "The tide keeps washing her down. Could you pull a little stronger?"

"Not without swamping the boat," said he. "You must bear up, sir, if you please—bear up until you see you're gaining. If once we drop to leeward of the landing place it's hard to say where we should get ashore, besides the chance of being boarded by the gigs; whereas, the way we go the current must slacken, and then we can dodge back along the shore."

"The current's less a'ready, sir," said the man Gray, who was sitting in the foresheets; "you can ease her off a bit."

"Thank you, my man," said I, quite as if nothing had happened; for we had all made up our minds to treat him like one of ourselves.

Suddenly the captain spoke again, and I thought his voice was a little changed. "The gun!" said he. "Look astern!"

We had entirely forgotten the long nine; and there, to our horror, were the five rogues busy about her, getting off the stout tarpaulin cover under which she sailed. It flashed into my mind at the same moment that the round shot and the powder for the gun had been left behind, and a stroke with an ax would put it all into the possession of the evil ones aboard.

"Israel was Flint's gunner," said Gray, hoarsely.

I could hear, as well as see, that brandy-faced rascal, Israel Hands, plumping down a round shot on the deck.

"Who's the best shot?" asked the captain.

"Mr. Trelawney, out and away," said I.

"Mr. Trelawney, will you please pick me off one of these men, sir? Hands, if possible," said the captain.

Trelawney was as cool as steel. He looked to the priming of his gun.

"Now," cried the captain, "easy with that gun, sir, or you'll swamp the boat. All hands stand by to trim her when he aims."

The squire raised his gun, the rowing ceased, and we leaned over to the other side to keep the balance. They had the gun, by this time, slued round upon the swivel, and Hands, at the muzzle with the rammer, was the most exposed. However, we had no luck, for just as

Trelawney fired, down he stooped, and it was one of the other four who fell. The cry he gave was echoed, not only by his companions on board, but by a great number of voices from the shore, and looking in that direction I saw the other pirates trooping out from among the trees and tumbling into their places in the boats.

"Here come the gigs, sir," said I.

"Give way, then," cried the captain. "We mustn't mind if we swamp her now. If we can't get ashore, all's up."

"Only one of the gigs is being manned, sir," I added; "the crew of the other is most likely going round by shore to cut us off."

"They'll have a hot run, sir," returned the captain. "Jack ashore, you know. It's not them I mind; it's the round shot. Carpet bowls! My lady's maid couldn't miss. Tell us, Squire, when you see the match, and we'll hold water."

We had been making headway at a good pace for a boat so overloaded. We were now close in; thirty or forty strokes and we should beach her. The gig was no longer to be feared; the little point had already concealed it. The ebb tide, which had delayed us, was now delaying our assailants. The one source of danger was the gun.

"If I durst," said the captain, "I'd stop and pick off another man."

But it was plain that they meant nothing should delay their shot. They had never so much as looked at their fallen comrade, though he was not dead, and I could see him trying to crawl away.

"Ready!" cried the squire.

"Hold!" cried the captain, quick as an echo.

And he and Redruth backed with a great heave that sent her stern bodily under water. The report of the gun fell in at the same instant of time. This was the first that Jim Hawkins heard, the sound of the squire's shot not having reached him. Where the ball passed not one of us precisely knew, but I fancy it must have been over our heads, and the wind of it may have contributed to our disaster. At any rate the boat sank by the stern in three feet of water, leaving the captain and myself, facing each other on our feet. The other three took complete headers, and came up again, drenched and bubbling.

All our stores were at the bottom, and to make things worse, only two guns out of five remained in a state for service. Mine I had snatched from my knees and held over my head by a sort of instinct. As for the captain, he had carried his over his shoulder by a bandoleer, and, like a wise man, lock uppermost. The other three had gone down with the boat. To add to our concern we heard voices already drawing near in the woods along shore; and we had not only the danger of being cut off from the stockade in our half-crippled state, but the fear whether, if Hunter and Joyce were attacked by half a dozen, they would have the sense and conduct to stand firm.

With all this in our minds we waded ashore as fast as we could, leaving behind us a good half of all our powder and provisions.

We made our best speed across the strip of wood that now divided us from the stockade, and at every step the voices of the buccaneers rang nearer. Soon we could hear the cracking of the branches as they breasted across a bit of thicket.

I began to see we should have a brush for it in earnest, and looked to my priming. "Captain," said I, "Trelawney is the dead shot. Give him your gun; his own is useless."

They exchanged guns, and Trelawney, silent and cool as he had been since the beginning of the bustle, hung a moment on his heel to see that all was fit for service. At the same time, observing Gray to be unarmed, I handed him my cutlass.

Forty paces farther we came to the edge of the wood and saw the stockade in front of us. We struck the inclosure about the middle of the south side, and, almost at the same time, seven mutineers— Job Anderson, the boatswain, at their head—appeared in full cry at the southwestern corner. They paused, as if taken aback; and before they recovered not only the squire and I, but Hunter and Joyce from the blockhouse, had time to fire. The four shots did the business; one of the enemy fell, and the rest turned and plunged into the trees. After reloading, we walked down the outside of the palisade to see the fallen enemy. He was stone-dead—shot through the heart.

We began to rejoice over our success when just at that moment a ball whistled close past my ear, and Tom Redruth fell his length on the ground. I saw with half an eye that all was over with poor Tom. We were suffered without further molestation to get the old game-keeper hoisted over the stockade and carried, groaning and bleeding, into the log house.

Poor old fellow, he had not uttered one word of surprise, complaint or fear from the very beginning of our troubles. He had followed every order silently, doggedly, and well; he was the oldest of our party by a score of years; and now, sullen, old, serviceable servant, it was he that was to die. The squire dropped down beside him on his knees and kissed his hand, crying like a child.

"Be I going, Doctor?" he asked.

"Tom, my man," said I, "you're going home."

"I wish I had had a lick at them with the gun first," he replied.

"Tom," said the squire, "say you forgive me, won't you?"

"Would that be respectful like, from me to you, Squire?" was the answer. "Howsoever, so be it, amen!" And not long after, without another word, he passed away.

In the meantime the captain, whom I had observed to be wonder-fully swollen about the chest and pockets, had turned out various stores—the British colors, a Bible, a coil of stoutish rope, pen, ink, the logbook, and pounds of tobacco. He had found a longish fir tree lying felled and cleared, and with the help of Hunter he had set it up at the corner of the log house where the trunks crossed and made an angle. Then, climbing on the roof, he had run up the colors.

This seemed mightily to relieve him, but he had an eye on Tom's passage, for all that; and as soon as all was over came forward with another flag and reverently spread it on the body.

"Don't you take on, sir," he said, shaking the squire's hand. "All's well with him; no fear for a hand that's been shot down in his duty to captain and owner. It mayn't be good divinity, but it's a fact."

Then he pulled me aside. "Dr. Livesey," he said, "in how many weeks do you and the squire expect the consort?"

I told him it was a question, not of weeks, but of months; that if we were not back by the end of August, Blandly was to send to find us. "You can calculate for yourself," I said.

"Why, yes," returned the captain, scratching his head, "and making a large allowance, sir, for all the gifts of Providence, I should say we were pretty close-hauled."

"How do you mean?" I asked.

"It's a pity, sir, we lost that second load. That's what I mean," replied the captain. "As for powder and shot, we'll do. But the rations are short, very short."

Just then, with a roar and a whistle, a round shot passed high above the roof of the log house and plumped far beyond us in the wood.

"Oho!" said the captain. "Blaze away! You've little enough powder already, my lads."

At the second trial the aim was better, and the ball descended inside the stockade, scattering a cloud of sand, but doing no further damage.

"Captain," said the squire, "the house is quite invisible from the ship. It must be the flag they are aiming at. Would it not be wiser to take it in?"

"Strike my colors!" cried the captain. "Not I, sir"; and as soon as he had said the words, we all agreed with him. For it was not only stout, seamanly, good feeling; it was good policy besides, and showed our enemies that we despised their cannonade.

All through the evening they kept thundering away. Ball after ball flew over or fell short or kicked up the sand in the inclosure; but they had to fire so high that the shot fell dead and buried itself in the soft sand. We had no ricochet to fear.

"There is one good thing about all this," observed the captain; "the wood in front of us is likely clear. The ebb has made a good while; our stores should be uncovered. Volunteers to go and bring in pork."

Gray and Hunter were the first to come forward. Well armed, they stole out of the stockade; but it proved a useless mission. The mutineers were bolder than we fancied. For four or five of them were busy carrying off our stores and wading out with them to one of the gigs that lay close by. Silver was in the stern sheets in command; and every man of them was now provided with a musket from some secret magazine of their own.

The captain sat down to his log, and here is the beginning of the entry:

> Alexander Smollett, master; David Livesey, ship's doctor; Abraham Gray, carpenter's mate; John Trelawney, owner; John Hunter and Richard Joyce, owner's servants, landsmen—being all that is left faithful to the ship's company—with stores for ten days at short rations, came ashore this day, and flew British colors on the log house in Treasure Island. Thomas Redruth, owner's servant, lands- man, shot by the mutineers; James Hawkins, cabin boy—

And at the same time I was wondering over poor Jim's fate.

A hail on the land side. "Doctor! Squire! Captain! Hullo, Hunter, is that you?" came the cries. I ran to the door in time to see Jim Hawkins, safe and sound, come climbing over the stockade.

IX. NARRATIVE RESUMED BY JIM HAWKINS: THE GARRISON IN THE STOCKADE

As soon as Ben Gunn saw the colors he stopped me by the arm, and sat down. "Now, said he, "there's your friends, sure enough."

"Far more likely it's the mutineers," I answered.

"Why," he cried, "in a place like this, Silver would fly the Jolly Roger. No, that's your friends. And here they are in the stockade as was made years ago by Flint. Ah, he was the man to have a headpiece, was Flint! Barring rum, his match were never seen. He was afraid of none, on'y Silver—Silver was that genteel."

"Well," said I, "that may be so; all the more reason that I should hurry on and join my friends."

"Nay, mate," returned Ben, "rum wouldn't bring me there, where you're going—not rum wouldn't, till I see your born gen'leman and gets it on his word of honor. And you won't forget my words!

'A precious sight' (that's what you'll say), 'a precious sight more confidence'—and then nips him."

And he pinched me again with the same air of cleverness.

"And when Ben Gunn is wanted, you know where to find him, Jim. Just wheer you found him today. Oh! and you'll say this: 'Ben Gunn,' says you, 'has reasons of his own.'"

"Well," said I, "I believe I understand. You have something to propose, and you wish to see the squire or the doctor; and you're to be found where I found you. Is that all?"

"And when? says you," he added. "Why, from about noon observation to about six bells."

"Good," said I; "and now may I go?"

"You won't forget?" he inquired, anxiously. "Precious sight, and reasons of his own, says you. And, Jim, if you was to see Silver, you wouldn't go for to sell Ben Gunn? No, says you. And if them pirates camp ashore, Jim, what would you say but there'd be widders in the morning?" Here he was interrupted by a loud report, and a cannon-ball came tearing through the trees and pitched in the sand not a hundred yards from where we two were talking. The next moment each of us had taken to his heels in a different direction.

For a good hour frequent reports shook the island and balls kept crashing through the woods. I moved from hiding place to hiding place, always pursued, or so it seemed to me, by these ter-rifying missiles. But after a long detour to the east I crept down among the shoreside trees.

The sun had just set; and the air, after the heat of the day, chilled me through my jacket. The *Hispaniola* still lay where she had anchored; but the Jolly Roger—the black flag of piracy—was flying from her peak. Even as I looked there was a red flash and one more round shot whistled through the air. It was the last of the cannonade.

I lay for some time, watching the bustle which succeeded the at-tack. Men were demolishing something with axes on the beach; the poor jolly boat, I afterward discovered. Away, near the mouth of the river, a great fire was glowing among the trees, and between that point and the ship one of the gigs kept coming and going, the men shouting at the oars like children. But there was a sound in their voices which suggested rum.

At length I thought I might return toward the stockade. As I rose to my feet I saw, some distance further down the spit, an isolated rock, high and peculiarly white in color. It occurred to me that this might be the white rock of which Ben Gunn had spoken, and that someday, if a boat were wanted, I should know where to look for one.

Then I skirted among the woods until I regained the stockade, and was warmly welcomed by the faithful party.

I had soon told my story, and began to look about me. The log house was made of unsquared trunks of pine—roof, walls, and floor. The latter stood in several places as much as a foot above the surface of the sand. There was a porch at the door, and under this porch the little spring welled up into an artificial basin of a rather odd kind— no other than a great ship's kettle of iron, with the bottom knocked out, and sunk "to her bearings," as the captain said, among the sand.

Little had been left beside the framework of the house; but inside in one corner there was a stone slab laid down by way of hearth and an old rusty iron basket to contain the fire. The cold evening breeze whistled through every chink of the rude building. Our chimney was a square hole in the roof; only a little part of the smoke found its way out, and the rest eddied about the house and kept us coughing and piping the eye. Add to this that Gray, the new man, had his face tied up in a bandage for the cut he had got in breaking away from the mutineers; and that poor old Tom Redruth, still unburied, lay along the wall, stiff and stark, under the Union Jack.

If we had been allowed to sit idle we should all have fallen into the blues, but Captain Smollett was never the man for that. All hands were called up before him, and he divided us into watches. The doctor and Gray and I for one; the squire, Hunter, and Joyce upon the other. Tired as we all were, two were sent out for firewood; two more were set to dig a grave for Redruth; the doctor was named cook; I was put sentry at the door; and the captain himself went from one to another, keeping up our spirits, and lending a hand wherever it was wanted.

From time to time the doctor came to the door to rest his eyes, which were almost smoked out of his head. "That man Smollett," he said, "is a better man than I am."

Another time he came and was silent for a while. Then he put his head on one side and said, "Is this Ben Gunn a man?"

"I do not know, sir," said I. "I am not very sure whether he's sane."

"A man who has been three years biting his nails on a desert island, Jim, can't expect to appear as sane as you or me," returned the doctor. "Was it cheese you said he had a fancy for?"

"Yes, sir, cheese," I answered.

"Well, Jim," says he, "just see the good that comes of being dainty in your food. You've seen my snuffbox, haven't you? And you never saw me take snuff; the reason being that in my snuffbox I carry a piece of Parmesan cheese—a cheese made in Italy, very nutritious. Well, that's for Ben Gunn!"

Before supper we buried old Tom in the sand, and stood round him for a while bareheaded in the breeze. Then, when we had eaten our pork, and each had a good stiff glass of brandy grog, the three chiefs got together in a corner to discuss our prospects.

They were at their wits' end what to do, the stores being so low that we must have been starved into surrender long before help came. But our best hope, it was decided, was to kill off the buccaneers until they either hauled down their flag or ran away with the *Hispaniola*. From nineteen they were already reduced to fifteen, two of whom were wounded, and one, at least—the man shot beside the gun— severely wounded, if he were not dead. And, besides that, we had two able allies—rum and the climate.

As for the first, though we were about half a mile away, we could hear them roaring and singing late into the night; and as for the second, the doctor staked his wig that, camped where they were in the marsh and unprovided with remedies, the half of them would be on their backs before a week. "So," he added, "if we are not all shot down first they'll be glad to be packing in the schooner."

"First ship that ever I lost," said Captain Smollett.

I was dead tired, as you may fancy; and when I got to sleep I slept like a log of wood. The rest had already breakfasted when I was awakened by a bustle and the sound of voices.

"Flag of truce!" I heard someone say; and then, "Silver himself!" And at that up I jumped and ran to a loophole in the wall.

Sure enough, two men were just outside the stockade, one of them waving a white cloth, the other, Silver himself, standing placidly by.

"Keep indoors, men," said the captain. "Ten to one this is a trick." Then he hailed the buccaneer. "Who goes? Stand, or we fire."

"Flag of truce," cried Silver.

The captain was in the porch, keeping himself out of the way of a treacherous shot should any be intended. He turned to us: "Doctor's watch on the lookout. Dr. Livesey take the north side, if you please; Jim, the east; Gray, west. The watch below, all hands to load muskets. Lively, men, and careful." Then he turned again to the mutineers. "And what do you want with your flag of truce?" he cried.

This time it was the other man who replied: "Cap'n Silver, sir, to come on board and make terms," he shouted.

"Cap'n Silver! Who's he?" cried the captain. And we could hear him adding to himself: "Cap'n, is it? Now here's promotion!"

Long John answered for himself. "Me, sir. These poor lads have chosen me cap'n, after your desertion, sir"—laying a particular emphasis upon the word "desertion." "We're willing to submit, if we can come to terms, and no bones about it. All I ask is your word to let me safe and sound out of this here stockade, and one minute to get out o' shot before a gun is fired."

"My man," said Captain Smollett, "I have not the slightest desire to talk to you. If you wish to talk to me, you can come, that's all. If there's any treachery, it'll be on your side, and the Lord help you."

"A word from you's enough, Cap'n," shouted Long John, cheerily. "I know a gentleman, and you may lay to that." Then he advanced to the stockade, threw over his crutch, got a leg up, and succeeded in surmounting the fence and dropping safely to the other side.

I will confess that I was not the slightest use as sentry; indeed, I had already deserted my eastern loophole and crept up behind the captain, who had now seated himself on the threshold, with his elbows on his knees, his head in his hands, and his eyes fixed on the water as it bubbled out of the old iron kettle in the sand. He was whistling to himself, "Come, Lasses and Lads."

Silver had terrible hard work getting up the knoll, what with the steepness of the incline and the soft sand. But he stuck to it like a man, and at last arrived before the captain, whom he saluted in the handsomest style. He was tricked out in his best coat, thick with brass buttons, and a fine laced hat was set on the back of his head.

"Here you are, my man," said the captain, raising his head. "You had better sit down."

"You ain't a-going to let me inside, Cap'n?" complained Long John. "It's a main cold morning, sir, to sit outside upon the sand."

"Why, Silver," said the captain, "if you had been an honest man you might have been sitting in your galley. It's your own doing. You're either my ship's cook—and then you were treated handsome—or Cap'n Silver, a common mutineer and pirate, and then you can go hang!"

"Well, well, Cap'n," returned the sea cook, sitting down on the sand, "you'll have to give me a hand up again, that's all. A sweet, pretty place you have of it here. Ah, there's Jim! The top of the morning to you, Jim. Doctor, here's my service. Why, there you all are like a happy family, in a manner of speaking."

"If you have anything to say, better say it," said the captain.

"Right you were, Cap'n Smollett," replied Silver. "Dooty is dooty, to be sure. Well, now, you look here, that was a good lay of yours last night. Some of you pretty handy with a handspike end. And I'll not deny but what some of my people was shook—maybe I was shook myself; maybe that's why I'm here for terms. But you mark me, Cap'n, it won't do twice, by thunder! We'll have to do sentry-go, and ease off a point or so on the rum. If I'd awoke a second sooner I'd 'a' caught you, I would. He wasn't dead when I got round to him, not he."

"Well?" says Captain Smollett, as cool as can be.

All that Silver said was a riddle to him, but you would never have guessed it from his tone. As for me, I began to have an inkling. Ben Gunn's last words came back to my mind. I began to suppose that he had paid the buccaneers a visit while they all lay drunk together round their fire, and I reckoned up with glee that we had only fourteen enemies to deal with.

"Well, here it is," said Silver. "We want that treasure, and we'll have it—that's our point! You would just as soon save your lives, I reckon; and that's yours. You have a chart, haven't you?"

"That's as may be," replied the captain.

"Oh, well, you have, I know that. You needn't be so husky with a man; there ain't a particle of service in that, and you may lay to it. Now, I never meant you no harm, myself."

"That won't do with me, my man," interrupted the captain. "We know exactly what you meant to do, and we don't care; for now, you see, you can't do it." And the captain looked at him calmly, and proceeded to fill a pipe.

"If Abe Gray—" Silver broke out.

"Avast there!" cried Mr. Smollett. "Gray told me nothing and I asked him nothing; and what's more I would see you and him and this whole island blown clean out of the water into blazes first."

This little whiff of temper seemed to cool Silver down. He had been growing nettled before, but now he pulled himself together. "Like enough," said he. "And, seein' as how you are about to take a pipe, Cap'n, I'll make so free as to do likewise."

And he filled a pipe and lighted it; and the two men sat silently smoking for a while, now looking each other in the face, now stopping their tobacco, now leaning forward to spit. It was as good as the play to see them.

"Now," resumed Silver, "here it is. You give us the chart to get the treasure by, and drop shooting poor seamen, and stoving of their heads in while asleep. You do that, and we'll offer you a choice. Either you come aboard along of us, once the treasure's shipped, and then I'll give you my affydavy, upon my word of honor, to clap you somewhere safe ashore. Or, if that ain't to your fancy, some of my hands being rough and having old scores, on account of hazing, then you can stay here, you can. We'll divide stores with you, man for man; and I'll give my affydavy, as before, to speak the first ship I sight, and send 'em here to pick you up. Now you'll own that's talking. Handsomer you couldn't look to get, not you. And I hope"—raising his voice—"that all hands in this here blockhouse will overhaul my words, for what is spoke to one is spoke to all."

Captain Smollett rose and knocked out the ashes of his pipe in the palm of his left hand. "Is that all?" he asked.

"Every last word, by thunder!" answered John. "Refuse that, and you've seen the last of me but musket balls."

"Very good," said the captain. "Now you'll hear me. If you come up one by one, unarmed, I'll engage to clap you all in irons and take you home to a fair trial in England. If you won't, my name is Alexander Smollett, I've flown my sovereign's colors, and I'll see you all to Davy Jones. You can't find the treasure. There's not a man among you fit to sail the ship. You can't fight us—Gray, there, got away from five of you. Your ship's in irons, Master Silver; you're on a lee shore, and so you'll find. I stand here and tell you so; and they're the last good words you'll get from me, for, in the name of Heaven, I'll put a bullet in your back when next I meet you. Tramp, my lad. Bundle out of this, please, hand over hand, and double quick."

Silver's face was a picture; his eyes started in his head with wrath. He shook the fire out of his pipe. "Give me a hand up!" he cried.

Not a man among us moved. Growling the foulest imprecations, he crawled along the sand till he got hold of the porch and could hoist himself again upon his crutch. Then he spat into the spring.

"There," he cried, "that's what I think of ye. Before an hour's out, I'll stove in your old blockhouse like a rum puncheon. Them that die'll be the lucky ones."

And with a dreadful oath he stumbled off, plowed down the sand, was helped across the stockade by the man with the flag of truce, and disappeared among the trees.

X. THE ATTACK

As soon as Silver disappeared, the captain turned back to find not a man of us at his post but Gray. It was the first time we had ever seen him angry.

"Quarters!" he roared. And then, as we all slunk back to our places, "Gray," he said, "I'll put your name in the log; you've stood by your duty like a seaman. Mr. Trelawney, I'm surprised at you, sir. Doctor, I thought you had worn the king's coat! If that was how you served at Fontenoy, sir, you'd have been better in your berth."

The doctor's watch were all back at their loopholes, the rest were busy loading the spare muskets, and everyone with a red face, you may be certain. The captain looked on for a while in silence. Then he spoke.

"My lads, I've given Silver a broadside; and before the hour's out, as he said, we shall be boarded. We're outnumbered, but we fight in shelter; and, a minute ago, I should have said we fought with discipline. I've no manner of doubt that we can drub them, if you choose." Then he went the rounds, and saw, as he said, that all was clear.

On the two short sides of the house, east and west, there were only two loopholes, on the south side where the porch was, two again; and on the north side, five. There was a round score of muskets for the seven of us; the firewood had been built into four piles—tables, you might say—one about the middle of each side, and on each of these tables some ammunition and four loaded muskets were laid ready to hand. In the middle the cutlasses lay ranged.

"Toss out the fire," said the captain; "the chill is past, and we mustn't have smoke in our eyes." The iron fire basket was carried out by Mr. Trelawney, and the embers smothered among sand.

"Hawkins hasn't had his breakfast. Hawkins, help yourself, and back to your post to eat it," continued Captain Smollett. "Hunter, serve out a round of brandy to all hands."

And while this was going on the captain completed the plan of the defense. "Doctor, you will take the door. See, and don't expose yourself; keep within, and fire through the porch. Hunter, take the east side. Joyce, you stand by the west. Mr. Trelawney, you are the best shot—you and Gray will take this long north side, with the five loopholes; it's there the danger is. Hawkins, neither you nor I are much account at the shooting; we'll stand by to load and bear a hand."

Soon the sun had climbed above our girdle of trees, and soon the sand was baking. Jackets were flung aside and we stood, each at his post, in a fever of heat and anxiety. An hour passed away. "Hang them!" said the captain. "This is as dull as the doldrums."

And just at that moment came the first news of the attack.

"If you please, sir," said Joyce, "if I see anyone am I to fire?"

"I told you so!" cried the captain.

"Thank you, sir," returned Joyce, with the same quiet civility.

Nothing followed for a time, till suddenly Joyce whipped up his musket and fired. The report had scarcely died away ere it was repeated and repeated from without in a scattering volley from every side of the inclosure. Several bullets struck the log house, but not one entered; and as the smoke cleared away, the stockade and the woods around it looked as quiet and empty as before.

"Did you hit your man?" asked the captain.

"No, sir," replied Joyce. "I believe not, sir."

"Next best thing to tell the truth," muttered Captain Smollett. "Load his gun, Hawkins. How many should you say there were on your side, Doctor?"

"I know precisely," said Dr. Livesey. "Three shots were fired on this side. I saw the three flashes."

"And how many on yours, Mr. Trelawney?"

But this was not so easily answered. There had come many from the north—seven, by the squire's computation; eight or nine, according to Gray. It was plain, therefore, that the attack would be developed from the north, and that on the other three sides we were only to be annoyed by a show of hostilities. But Captain Smollett made no change in his arrangements. If the mutineers succeeded in crossing

the stockade, he argued, they would take possession of any unprotected loophole, and shoot us down like rats in our own stronghold.

Nor had we much time left for thought. Suddenly, with a loud
huzza, a little cloud of pirates leaped from the woods on the north
side, and ran straight on the stockade. At the same moment the fire
was once more opened from the woods and a rifle ball sang through
the doorway and knocked the doctor's musket into bits.

The boarders swarmed over the fence like monkeys. Squire and
Gray fired again and yet again; three men fell, one forward into the
inclosure, two back on the outside. But of these, one was on his feet
again in a crack and instantly disappeared among the trees. Four had
made good their footing inside our defenses, while from the shelter
of the woods seven or eight men, each evidently supplied with several
muskets, kept up a hot though useless fire on the log house.

The four who had boarded made straight for the building, shouting
as they ran. In a moment, they had swarmed up the mound and were
upon us. The head of Job Anderson, the boatswain, appeared at the
middle loophole. "At 'em, all hands—all hands!" he roared.

At the same moment another pirate grasped Hunter's musket by
the muzzle, wrenched it from his hands, and with one stunning blow
laid the poor fellow senseless on the floor. Meanwhile a third, running
unharmed all round the house, appeared suddenly in the doorway
and fell with his cutlass on the doctor.

Our position was utterly reversed. A moment since we were firing,
under cover, at an exposed enemy; now it was we who lay uncovered,
and could not return a blow. The log house was full of smoke, to
which we owed our comparative safety. Cries and confusion, the
flashes and reports of pistol shots, and one loud groan, rang in my ears.

"Out, lads, out, and fight 'em in the open! Cutlasses!" cried the
captain. I snatched a cutlass, and someone at the same time snatched
another, giving me a cut across the knuckles which I hardly felt. I
dashed out of the door into the sunlight. Someone was close behind, I
knew not whom. Right in front, the doctor was pursuing his assailant
down the hill, and, just as my eyes fell upon him, beat down his guard,

and sent him sprawling on his back with a great slash across the face.

"Round the house, lads!" cried the captain; and even in the hurly-burly I perceived a change in his voice. Mechanically I obeyed, and, with my cutlass raised, ran round the corner of the house. Next moment I was face to face with Anderson. He roared aloud, and his hanger went up above his head, flashing in the sunlight. As the blow still hung impending, I leaped in a trice upon one side, and, missing my foot in the soft sand, rolled headlong down the slope.

When I had first sallied from the door the other mutineers had been swarming up the palisade to make an end of us. One man, in a red nightcap, with his cutlass in his mouth, had even got upon the top and thrown a leg across. Well, when I found my feet again, the fellow with the red nightcap was still halfway over. And yet, in this breath of time, the fight was over and the victory was ours.

Gray, following close behind me, had cut down the big boatswain ere he had time to recover from his lost blow. Another had been shot at a loophole in the very act of firing into the house, and now lay in agony, the pistol still smoking in his hand. A third, as I had seen, the doctor had disposed of at a blow. Of the four who had scaled the palisade, one only remained unaccounted for, and he was now clambering out again with the fear of death upon him.

"Fire—fire from the house!" cried the doctor. "And you, lads, back into cover." But his words were unheeded, no shot was fired, and the last boarder made good his escape. In three seconds nothing remained of the attacking party but the five who had fallen, four on the inside, and one on the outside of the palisade.

The doctor and Gray and I ran full speed for shelter. The survivors would soon be back, and at any moment the fire might recommence. The house was by this time somewhat cleared of smoke, and we saw at a glance the price we had paid for victory. Hunter lay beside his loophole, stunned; Joyce by his, shot through the head, never to move again; and the squire was supporting the captain, one as pale as the other.

"The captain's wounded," said Mr. Trelawney.

"Have they run?" asked Mr. Smollett.

"All that could, you may be bound," returned the doctor; "but there's five of them will never run again."

"Five!" cried the captain. "Come, that's better odds than we had at starting. Five lost against three leaves us four to nine. We were seven to nineteen then—or thought we were, and that's as bad to bear."*

XI. HOW I BEGAN MY SEA ADVENTURE

THERE WAS NO RETURN of the mutineers, and we had a quiet time to overhaul the wounded. Out of the eight men who had fallen in the action only three still breathed—that pirate who had been shot at the loophole, Hunter, and Captain Smollett; and of these the first two were as good as dead; the mutineer, indeed, died under the doctor's knife, and Hunter never recovered consciousness. As for the captain, his wounds were grievous, but not dangerous. Anderson's ball—for it was Job that shot him first—had broken his shoulder blade and touched the lung, not badly; the second had only torn some muscles in the calf. He was sure to recover, the doctor said, but for weeks to come he must not walk nor move his arm, nor so much as speak when he could help it.

After dinner the squire and the doctor sat by the captain's side awhile in consultation; and when they had talked to their hearts' content, it being then a little past noon, the doctor took up his hat and pistols, girt on a cutlass, put the chart in his pocket, and, with a musket on his shoulder, crossed the palisade on the north side and set off briskly through the trees.

Gray and I were sitting together at the far end of the blockhouse, to be out of earshot of our officers consulting; and Gray took his pipe out of his mouth and fairly forgot to put it back again, so thunderstruck he was at this occurrence.

---

*The mutineers were soon only eight in number, for the man shot by Mr. Trelawney on board the schooner died that same evening of his wound. But this was, of course, not known till after by the faithful party.

"In the name of Davy Jones," said he, "is Dr. Livesey mad?"

"Why, no," says I. "He's about the last of this crew for that. I take it he's going now to see Ben Gunn."

I was right, as appeared later; but in the meantime, the house being stifling hot and the palisade ablaze with midday sun, I began to get another thought into my head which was not by any means so right. What I began to do was to envy the doctor, walking in the cool woods while I sat grilling, with my clothes stuck to the hot resin, and so many poor dead bodies lying around that I took a disgust of the place that was almost as strong as fear.

All the time I was washing out the blockhouse this disgust and envy kept growing stronger and stronger, till at last, being near a bread bag, I took the first step toward my escapade and filled both pockets of my coat with biscuit. The next thing I laid hold of was a brace of pistols; I already had a powder horn and bullets.

As for the scheme I had in my head, it was not a bad one in itself. I was to go down the sandy spit that divided the anchorage on the east from the open sea, find the white rock I had observed last evening, and ascertain whether it was there that Ben Gunn had hidden his boat; a thing quite worth doing, as I still believe. But as I was certain I should not be allowed to leave the inclosure, my plan was to slip out when nobody was watching; and that was so bad a way of doing it as made the thing itself wrong. But I was only a boy, and I had made my mind up.

Well, as things fell out, I found an admirable opportunity. The squire and Gray were busy helping the captain with his bandages; the coast was clear; I made a bolt for it over the stockade and into the thickest of the trees.

I took my way straight for the east coast of the island, for I was determined to go down the sea side of the spit to avoid all chance of observation from the anchorage. It was already late in the afternoon, although still warm and sunny. As I continued to thread the tall woods I could hear from far before me the thunder of the surf, and soon cool draughts of air began to reach me from the sea breezes.

A few steps farther I came forth into the open borders of the grove, and saw the sea lying blue and sunny to the horizon.

I have never seen the sea quiet round Treasure Island. The sun might blaze overhead, the air be without a breath, the surface smooth, but still these great rollers would be running along all the external coast, thundering and thundering by day and night; and I scarce believe there is one spot in the island where a man would be out of earshot of their noise.

I walked along beside the surf with great enjoyment till, thinking I was now got far enough to the south, I took the cover of some thick bushes and crept warily up to the ridge of the spit. Behind me was the sea; in front the anchorage lay still and leaden as when first we entered it. The *Hispaniola*, in that unbroken mirror, was exactly portrayed from the trunk to the waterline, the Jolly Roger hanging from her peak. Alongside lay one of the gigs, Silver in the stern sheets, while a couple of men were leaning over the stern bulwarks, one of them with a red cap—the very rogue that I had seen some hours before stride-legs upon the palisade. All at once there began the most horrid, unearthly screaming, which at first startled me badly, though I soon had remembered the voice of Captain Flint, and even thought I could make out the bird by her bright plumage as she sat perched upon her master's wrist.

Soon the gig shoved off and pulled for shore. Just about the same time the sun had gone down behind the Spy-glass, and I saw I must lose no time if I were to find the boat that evening.

The white rock, visible above the brush, was still some eighth of a mile farther down the spit, and it took me a goodish while to get up with it, crawling, often on all fours, among the scrub. Night had almost come when I laid my hand on its rough sides. Right below it there was a small hollow of green turf, hidden by a thick underwood; and in the center of the dell, sure enough, a little tent of goatskins, like what the gypsies carry about with them in England.

I dropped into the hollow, lifted the side of the tent, and there was Ben Gunn's boat—a rude, lopsided framework of tough wood, and stretched upon that a covering of goatskin, with the hair inside. There was one thwart set as low as possible, a kind of stretcher in the bows, and a double paddle for propulsion. The thing was extremely small, even for me; but one great advantage the coracle certainly possessed, for it was exceedingly light and portable.

Well, now that I had found the boat, you would have thought I had had enough of truantry for once; but in the meantime I had taken another notion. This was to slip out at night, cut the *Hispaniola* adrift, and let her go ashore where she fancied. I had quite made up my mind that the mutineers had nothing nearer their hearts than to up anchor and away to sea; this, I thought, it would be a fine thing to prevent; and now that I had seen how they left their watchmen unprovided with a boat, I thought it might be done with little risk.

Down I sat to wait for darkness, and made a hearty meal of biscuit. It was a night out of ten thousand for my purpose. The fog had now buried all heaven, and when at last I shouldered the coracle and groped my way out of the hollow there were but two points visible on the whole anchorage.

One was the great fire on shore, by which the defeated pirates lay carousing in the swamp. The other, a mere blur of light upon the darkness, indicated the position of the anchored ship. She had swung round to the ebb—her bow was now toward me—the only lights on board were in the cabin; and what I saw was merely a reflection on the fog of the strong rays that flowed from the stern window.

The ebb had already run some time, and I had to wade through a long belt of swampy sand before I came to the edge of the retreating water and, wading in, set my coracle on the surface.

The coracle—as I had ample reason to know before I was done with her—was a very safe boat for a person of my height and weight, both buoyant and clever in a seaway; but she was the most cross-grained, lopsided craft to manage. She turned in every direction but the one I was bound to go; the most part of the time we were broadside on, and I am sure I never should have made the ship but for the tide. By good fortune, paddle as I pleased, the tide was still sweeping me down; and there lay the *Hispaniola* right in the fairway, hardly to be missed.

First she loomed before me like a blot of something yet blacker than darkness, then her spars and hull began to take shape, and the next moment, as it seemed (for the farther I went the brisker grew the current of the ebb), I was alongside of her hawser and had laid hold.

The hawser was as taut as a bowstring—so strong she pulled upon her anchor. All round the hull the rippling current bubbled and chattered like a little mountain stream. One cut with my sea gully and the *Hispaniola* would go humming down the tide.

So far so good; but it next occurred to my recollection that a taut hawser, suddenly cut, is a thing as dangerous as a kicking horse. Ten to one, if I were so foolhardy as to cut the *Hispaniola* from her anchor, I and the coracle would be knocked clean out of the water.

But just while I was meditating, the light airs which had begun blowing from the southeast hauled round into the southwest. A puff came, caught the *Hispaniola*, and forced her up into the current; and, to my great joy, I felt the hawser slacken in my grasp, and the hand by which I held it dip for a second under water. With that I took out my gully, opened it with my teeth, and cut one strand after another, till the vessel only swung by two. Then I lay quiet, waiting to sever these last when the strain should be once more lightened by a breath of wind.

All this time I had heard loud voices from the cabin; but, to say truth, my mind had been so entirely taken up with other thoughts that I had scarcely given ear. Now, however, I recognized one for the coxswain's, Israel Hands, that had been Flint's gunner in former days. The other was my friend of the red nightcap. Both men were plainly the worse for drink, and furiously angry. Oaths flew like hailstones, and now and then there came forth such an explosion as I thought was sure to end in blows. But each time the quarrel passed off, and the voices grumbled lower for a while, until the next crisis came.

At last the breeze came; the schooner sidled and drew nearer in the dark; I felt the hawser slacken once more, and, with a good tough effort, cut the last fibers through. The breeze had but little action on the coracle, and I was almost instantly swept by the tide against the bows of the *Hispaniola*. At the same time the schooner began to turn upon her heel, spinning slowly, end for end, across the current.

I wrought like a fiend, for I expected every moment to be swamped; and since I found I could not push the coracle directly off, I now shoved straight astern. At length I was clear of my dangerous neighbor; and just as I gave the last impulsion my hands came across a light cord that was trailing overboard across the stern bulwarks. Instantly I grasped it.

Why I should have done so I can hardly say. It was at first mere instinct; but once I had it in my hands, and found it fast, curiosity began to get the upper hand, and I determined I should have one look through the cabin window. I pulled in hand over hand on the cord, and when I judged myself near enough rose at infinite risk to about half my height, and thus commanded the roof and a slice of the interior of the cabin.

By this time the schooner and her little consort were gliding pretty swiftly through the anchorage; indeed, we had fetched up level with the campfire. The ship was talking, as sailors say, loudly, treading the innumerable ripples with an incessant weltering splash; and until I got my eye above the windowsill I could not comprehend why the watchman had taken no alarm. One glance, however, was sufficient; and it was only one glance that I durst take from that unsteady skiff. It showed me Hands and his companion locked together in deadly wrestle, each with a hand upon the other's throat.

I dropped upon the thwart again, none too soon, for I was surprised by a sudden lurch of the coracle. At the same moment she yawed sharply and seemed to change her course. The speed, in the meantime, had strangely increased. The *Hispaniola* herself, a few yards in whose wake I was still being whirled along, seemed to stagger in her course, and I saw her spars toss a little against the blackness of the night; nay, as I looked longer, I made sure she also was wheeling to the southward.

I glanced over my shoulder, and my heart jumped against my ribs. There, right behind me, was the glow of the pirates' campfire. I could hear the men's voices break into the doleful chorus I had heard so often:

"Fifteen men on the Dead Man's Chest—
Yo-ho-ho, and a bottle of rum;
Drink and the devil had done for the rest—
Yo-ho-ho, and a bottle of rum!"

I was just thinking how busy drink and the devil were at that very moment in the cabin of the *Hispaniola* when I realized the current had turned at right angles, sweeping round along with it the tall schooner and the little dancing coracle; ever quickening, ever bubbling higher, ever muttering louder, it went spinning through the narrows for the open sea.

Suddenly the schooner gave a violent yaw, turning, perhaps, through twenty degrees; and almost at the same moment one shout followed another from on board; I could hear feet pounding on the companion ladder, and I knew that the two drunkards had at last been interrupted in their quarrel and awakened to a sense of their disaster.

I lay down flat in the bottom of that wretched skiff and devoutly recommended my spirit to its Maker. At the end of the straits I made sure we must fall into some bar of raging breakers, where all my troubles would be ended speedily.

So I must have lain for hours, continually beaten to and fro upon the billows, and never ceasing to expect death at the next plunge. Gradually weariness grew upon me, even in the midst of my terrors, until sleep at last supervened, and in my sea-tossed coracle I lay and dreamed of home and the old Admiral Benbow.

IT WAS BROAD DAY when I awoke and found myself tossing at the southwest end of Treasure Island. Haulbowline Head and Mizzenmast Hill were at my elbow. I was scarce a quarter of a mile to seaward, and it was my first thought to paddle in and land.

That notion was soon given over. Among great masses of fallen rocks the breakers spouted and bellowed; and I saw myself, if I ventured nearer, dashed to death upon the rough shore. I had a better chance, as I supposed, before me. North of Haulbowline Head the land runs in a long way, leaving, at low tide, a stretch of yellow sand. To the north of that, again, there comes another cape—"Cape of ye Woods," as it was marked upon the chart—buried in tall green pines.

I remembered what Silver had said about the current that sets northward along the whole west coast of Treasure Island; and seeing from my position that I was already under its influence, I preferred to leave Haulbowline Head behind me, and reserve my strength for an attempt to land upon the kindlier looking Cape of the Woods.

There was a great, smooth swell upon the sea, and the billows rose and fell unbroken. Often, as I still lay at the bottom, I would see a big blue summit heaving close above me; yet the coracle would but bounce a little, dance as if on springs, and subside on the other side into the trough as lightly as a bird. I began after a little to grow bold, and sat up to try my skill at paddling. But I had hardly moved before the boat, giving up at once her gentle dancing movement, ran straight down a slope of water and struck her nose, with a spout of spray, deep into the side of the next wave.

I was drenched and terrified, and fell instantly back into my old position, whereupon the coracle again led me as softly as before among the billows. It was plain she was not to be interfered with, and since I could in no way influence her course, what hope had I left of reaching land? I began to be horribly frightened, but I kept my head. First, moving with all care, I gradually bailed out the coracle with my sea cap; then, getting my eye above the gunwale, I set myself to study how it was she managed to slip so quietly through the rollers. I found each wave, instead of the big, smooth, glossy mountain it looks from shore, or from a vessel's deck, was for all the world like any range of hills on the dry land, full of peaks and smooth places and valleys. The coracle, left to herself, turning from side to side, threaded, so to speak, her way through these lower parts, and avoided the steep slopes and higher, toppling summits of the wave.

"Well, now," thought I, "it is plain I must lie where I am, and not disturb the balance; but it is plain also that I can put the paddle over the side, and from time to time give her a shove toward land."

It was slow work, yet I did visibly gain ground; and, as we drew near the Cape of the Woods, though I saw I must miss that point, I felt sure I should make the next promontory. It was high time, for I now began to be tortured with thirst. The glow of the sun from above, its thousandfold reflection from the waves, the sea water that fell and dried upon me, caking my lips with salt, combined to make my throat burn and my brain to ache; but as the next reach of sea opened out, I beheld a sight that changed the nature of my thoughts.

Right in front of me, not half a mile away, I beheld the *Hispaniola* under sail. I made sure, of course, that I should be taken, but I was so in want of water that I scarce knew whether to be glad or sorry. Long before I had come to a conclusion, surprise had taken entire possession of my mind, and I could do nothing but stare and wonder.

The *Hispaniola* was under her mainsail and two jibs, and the beautiful white canvas shone in the sun like snow or silver. When I first sighted her she was lying a course about northwest; and I presumed the men on board were going round the island on their way back to the anchorage. Presently she began to fetch more to the westward, so that I thought they had sighted me and were going about in chase. At last, however, she fell right into the wind's eye, was taken dead aback, and stood there awhile helpless, with her sails shivering. Then she filled again upon another tack, sailed swiftly for a minute or so, and brought up once more dead in the wind's eye.

It became plain to me that nobody was steering. Either the men were dead-drunk or had deserted her, I thought, and perhaps if I could get on board I might return the vessel to her captain.

The current was bearing coracle and schooner northward at an equal rate. If only I dared to sit up and paddle, I could overhaul her. The scheme had an air of adventure that inspired me, and the thought of the water beaker beside the fore companion doubled my growing courage. Up I got and set myself, with all my strength and caution, to paddle after the unsteered *Hispaniola*. I was now gaining on the schooner; I could see the brass glisten on the tiller as it banged about; and still no soul appeared upon her decks.

The breeze fell very low and, the current gradually turning her, the *Hispaniola* revolved slowly round her center and at last presented me her stern, with the cabin window still gaping open and the lamp over the table still burning on into the day. The mainsail hung drooped like a banner. She was stock-still, but for the current. I was not a hundred yards from her when the wind came again in a clap; she filled on the port tack, and was off again, stooping and skimming like a swallow. My first impulse was one of despair, but my second was toward joy. Round she came till she was broadside on to me—round still till she had covered a half, and then two thirds, and then three quarters of the distance that separated us. I could see the waves boiling white under her forefoot.

And then of a sudden I began to comprehend. I had scarce time to act and save myself. I was on the summit of one swell when the schooner came swooping over the next. The bowsprit was over my head. I sprang to my feet and leaped, stamping the coracle under water. With one hand I caught the jib boom, while my foot was lodged between the stay and the brace; and as I clung there panting a dull blow told me that the schooner had struck the coracle, and that I was left without retreat on the *Hispaniola*.

XII. I STRIKE THE JOLLY ROGER

I HAD SCARCE GAINED a position on the bowsprit when the flying jib flapped and filled upon the other tack with a report like a gun. The schooner trembled to her keel under the reverse; but next moment, the other sails still drawing, the jib flapped back and hung idle. This had nearly tossed me off into the sea; and now I lost no time, crawled back along the bowsprit, and tumbled head foremost on the deck. I was on the lee side of the forecastle, and the mainsail concealed from me a certain portion of the afterdeck. Not a soul was to be seen. The planks bore the print of many feet; and an empty bottle, broken by the neck, tumbled to and fro in the scuppers.

Suddenly the *Hispaniola* came right into the wind. The jibs behind me cracked aloud; the rudder slammed to; the whole ship gave a sickening heave and shudder, and at the same moment the main boom swung inboard and showed me the lee afterdeck.

There were the two watchmen, sure enough; red-cap on his back, as still as a handspike, with his arms stretched out like those of a crucifix, and his teeth showing through his open lips; Israel Hands propped against the bulwarks, his chin on his chest, his face as white, under its tan, as a tallow candle.

For a while the ship kept bucking and sidling like a vicious horse, and at every jump of the schooner red-cap slipped to and fro; but— what was ghastly to behold—neither his attitude nor his fixed, teeth-disclosing grin was anyway disturbed by this rough usage. At every jump, too, Hands appeared still more to settle down upon the deck, his feet sliding ever the farther out, and the whole body canting toward the stern. I observed around both of them splashes of dark blood upon the planks, and began to feel sure that they had killed each other in their drunken wrath.

While I was thus looking and wondering, in a calm moment when the ship was still, Israel Hands turned partly round and, with a low moan, writhed himself back to the position in which I had seen him first. I walked aft until I reached the mainmast.

"Come aboard, Mr. Hands," I said, ironically.

He rolled his eyes round heavily, but he was too far gone to express surprise. All he could do was to utter one word—"Brandy."

It occurred to me there was no time to lose; and, dodging the boom as it once more lurched across the deck, I slipped aft and down the companion stairs into the cabin. It was such a scene of confusion as you can hardly fancy. All the lockfast places had been broken open in quest of the chart. The floor was thick with mud where ruffians had sat down to drink or consult after wading in the marshes round their camp. Empty bottles clinked together in corners to the rolling of the ship. One of the doctor's medical books lay open on the table, half of the leaves gutted out, I suppose, for pipe lights. In the midst of all this the lamp still cast a smoky glow, obscure and brown as umber.

I went into the cellar; all the barrels were gone, and of the bottles a most surprising number had been drunk out and thrown away. Certainly, since the mutiny began not a man of them could ever have been sober. Foraging about, I found a bottle with some brandy left, for Hands; and for myself I routed out some biscuit, some pickled fruits, a great bunch of raisins, and a piece of cheese. With these I came on deck, put down my own stock behind the rudderhead and went forward to the water beaker, and had a good deep drink of water, and only then gave Hands the brandy.

He must have drunk a gill before he took the bottle from his mouth. "Aye," said he, "by thunder, but I wanted that!"

I had sat down already in my own corner and begun to eat. "Much hurt?" I asked him.

He grunted, or rather I might say he barked. "If that doctor was aboard, I'd be right enough in a couple of turns; but I don't have no manner of luck, you see, and that's what's the matter with me. As for that swab, he's good as dead, he is," he added, indicating the man with the red cap. "He warn't no seaman, anyhow. And where mought you have come from?"

"Well," said I, "I've come aboard to take possession of this ship, Mr. Hands, and you'll please regard me as your captain until further notice." He looked at me sourly enough, but said nothing. "By-the-by," I continued, "I can't have these colors, Mr. Hands; and, by your leave, I'll strike 'em."

And, again dodging the boom, I ran to the color lines, handed down their cursed black flag, and chucked it overboard. "God save the king!" said I, waving my cap; "and there's an end to Captain Silver!"

He watched me keenly and slyly, his chin all the while on his breast. "I reckon," he said at last—"I reckon, Cap'n Hawkins, you'll kind of want to get ashore now. S'pose we talks."

"Why, yes," says I, "with all my heart, Mr. Hands. Say on." And I went back to my meal with a good appetite.

"This man," he began, nodding feebly at the corpse—"O'Brien were his name—a rank Irelander—this man and me got the canvas on her, meaning for to sail her back. Well, he's dead now, he is—as dead as bilge; and who's to sail this ship I don't see. Without I gives you a hint, you ain't that man, as far's I can tell. Now, look here, you gives me food and drink and a old scarf or 'ankercher to tie my wound up, you do, and I'll tell you how to sail her; and that's about square all round, I take it."

"I'll tell you one thing," says I: "I'm not going back to Captain Kidd's anchorage. I mean to get into North Inlet, and beach her quietly there."

"North Inlet?" he cried. "Why, I can see, can't I? I've tried my fling, and I've lost, and it's you has the wind of me. I haven't no ch'ice, not I! I'd help you sail her up to Execution Dock, by thunder!"

Well, as it seemed to me, there was some sense in this. We struck our bargain on the spot. In three minutes I had the *Hispaniola* sailing easily before the wind along the coast of Treasure Island, with good hopes of turning the northern point ere noon, and beating down again as far as North Inlet before high water. Then I lashed the tiller and went below to my own chest, where I got a soft silk handkerchief of my mother's. With this, and with my aid, Hands bound up the great bleeding stab he had received in the thigh, and after he had eaten a little and had a swallow or two more of the brandy he began to pick up visibly.

The breeze served us admirably. Soon we were past the high lands and bowling beside low, sandy country, and soon we were beyond that again, and had turned the corner of the rocky hill that ends the island on the north.

I was greatly elated with my new command. I had now plenty of water and good things to eat, and my conscience, which had smitten me hard for my desertion, was quieted by the great conquest I had made. I should, I think, have had nothing left me to desire but for the eyes of the coxswain as they followed me derisively about the deck, and the odd smile that appeared continually on his face as he craftily watched and watched and watched me at my work.

THE WIND, SERVING US to a desire, now hauled into the west. We could run so much the easier from the northeast corner of the island to the mouth of the North Inlet. Only, as we had no power to anchor, and dared not beach her till the tide had flowed a good deal farther, time hung on our hands. The coxswain told me how to lay the ship to; after a good many trials I succeeded, and we both sat in silence over another meal.

"Cap'n," said he, at length, with an uncomfortable smile, "I'll take it kind if you'd step down into that there cabin and get me a—well, a—bottle of wine. This here brandy's too strong for my head."

Now, the coxswain's hesitation seemed to be unnatural, and as for the notion of his preferring wine to brandy, I entirely disbelieved it. He wanted me to leave the deck—so much was plain; but with what purpose I could in no way imagine. I was prompt with my answer, however, for I saw where my advantage lay. "Some wine?" I said. "Will you have white or red?"

"Well, I reckon it's about the blessed same to me, shipmate."

"All right," I answered. "I'll bring you port, Mr. Hands. But I'll have to dig for it." With that I scuttled down the companion with all the noise I could, slipped off my shoes, ran quietly along the gallery, mounted the forecastle ladder, and popped my head cautiously out of the fore companion. The worst of my suspicions proved too true.

He had risen from his position to his hands and knees, and, though his leg obviously hurt him when he moved—for I could hear him stifle a groan—yet it was at a good rate that he trailed himself across the deck. In half a minute he had reached the port scuppers and picked, out of a coil of rope, a long knife, or rather a short dirk, discolored with blood. He tried the point upon his hand, and then, concealing it in the bosom of his jacket, trundled back into his old place against the bulwark.

This was all that I required to know. Israel could move about; he was now armed; and it was plain that I was meant to be the victim.

Yet I felt sure that I could trust him in one point, since in that our interests jumped together, and that was in the disposition of the schooner. We both desired to have her stranded safe enough, in a sheltered place, and so that, when the tide came, she could be got off again with as little labor and danger as might be; and until that was done I considered that my life would certainly be spared.

While I was thus turning the business over in my mind I had stolen back to the cabin, slipped once more into my shoes, and laid my hand at random on a bottle of wine; and now I made my reappearance on the deck.

Hands lay as I had left him, all fallen together in a bundle. He looked up, however, at my coming, knocked the neck off the bottle and took a good swig. Then he pulled out a stick of tobacco. "Cut me a junk o' that," says he, "for I haven't no knife and hardly strength enough, so be as I had. Ah, Jim, Jim, cut me a quid, as'll likely be the last; for I'm for my long home, and no mistake."

"Well," said I, "I'll cut you some tobacco; but if I was you and thought myself so badly I would go to my prayers, like a Christian."

"Why?" said he. "Now, you tell me why."

"Why?" I cried. "You've broken your trust; you've lived in sin and lies and blood; there's a man you killed lying at your feet this moment. For God's mercy, Mr. Hands, that's why."

I spoke with a little heat, thinking of the bloody dirk he had hidden to end me with. He, for his part, took a great draught of the wine and spoke with the most unusual solemnity. "For thirty years," he said, "I've sailed the seas, and seen good and bad, fair weather and foul, provisions running out, knives going, and what not. Well, now I tell you I never seen good come o' goodness yet. Him as strikes first is my fancy; dead men don't bite; them's my views—amen, so be it. And now," he added, changing his tone, "we've had enough of this foolery. The tide's made good enough by now. You just take my orders, Cap'n Hawkins, and we'll sail slap in and be done with it."

All told, we had scarce two miles to run, but the entrance to this northern anchorage was narrow and shoal, so that the schooner must be nicely handled to be got in. I think I was a good, prompt subaltern, and I am very sure that Hands was an excellent pilot, for we went about and about, shaving the banks with a certainty and a neatness that were a pleasure to behold.

Scarcely had we passed the heads before the land closed around us. Right before us we saw the wreck of a ship in the last stages of dilapidation. It had been a great vessel of three masts, but had lain so long exposed to the weather that it was hung about with great webs of dripping seaweed, and on the deck of it shore bushes had taken root and now flourished thick with flowers. It was a sad sight, but it showed us that the anchorage was calm.

"Now," said Hands, "look there; there's a pet bit for to beach a ship in. Fine flat sand, never a cat's-paw, and flowers a-blowing like a garding on that old ship."

"And once beached," I asked, "how shall we get her off again?"

"Why, so," he replied; "you take a line ashore there on the other side at low water; take a turn about one o' them big pines; bring it back, take a turn round the capstan, and lie to for the tide. Come high water, all hands pull upon the line, and off she comes as sweet as natur'. And now, boy, starboard a little—so—steady—starboard—larboard a little—steady—steady!"

So he issued his commands, which I breathlessly obeyed, till, all of a sudden, he cried, "Now, my hearty, luff!" And I put the helm hard up, and the *Hispaniola* swung round and ran stem on for the low wooded shore.

I was so much interested, waiting for the ship to touch, that I had quite forgot the peril that hung over my head, and stood craning over the starboard bulwarks and watching the ripples spreading wide before the bows. I might have fallen without a struggle had not a sudden disquietude made me turn my head. Perhaps it was an instinct like a cat's; but, sure enough, when I looked round, there was Hands, already halfway toward me, with the dirk in his right hand.

We must both have cried out aloud when our eyes met; but while mine was the shrill cry of terror, his was a roar like a charging bull's. At the same instant he threw himself forward, and I leaped sideways toward the bows. As I did so I left hold of the tiller, which sprang sharp to leeward; and this saved my life, for it struck Hands across the chest and stopped him, for the moment, dead.

Before he could recover I was safe out of the corner with all the deck to dodge about. Just forward of the mainmast I stopped, drew a pistol from my pocket, took a cool aim, though he was once more coming directly after me, and drew the trigger. The hammer fell, but there followed neither flash nor sound; the priming was useless with seawater, and I was now a mere fleeing sheep before this butcher.

Wounded as he was, it was wonderful how fast Hands could move in his fury. I had no time to try my other pistol, nor, indeed, much inclination, for I was sure it would be useless. One thing I saw plainly; I must not simply retreat before him or he would speedily hold me boxed into the bows, as a moment since he had so nearly boxed me in the stern. I placed my palms against the mainmast and waited, every nerve upon the stretch.

Seeing that I meant to dodge, he also paused; and a moment or two passed in feints on his part and corresponding movements upon mine. It was such a game as I had often played at home about the rocks of Black Hill Cove, but never before, you may be sure, with such a wildly beating heart as now. Still, as I say, it was a boy's game, and I thought I could hold my own at it against an elderly seaman with a wounded thigh.

Well, while things stood thus suddenly the *Hispaniola* struck, staggered, ground for an instant in the sand, and then, swift as a blow, canted over to the port side, till the deck stood at an angle of forty-five degrees.

We were both of us capsized in a second, and both rolled, almost together, into the scuppers; the dead red-cap, with his arms still spread out, tumbling stiffly after us. I was the first afoot, for Hands had got involved with the dead body. The sudden canting of the ship had made the deck no place for running on; I had to find some new way of escape, and that upon the instant. Quick as thought I sprang into the mizzen shrouds and did not draw a breath till I was seated on the crosstrees.

Now that I had a moment to myself I lost no time in changing the priming of my pistol, and then, to make assurance doubly sure, I proceeded to draw the load of the other and recharge it afresh.

My new employment struck Hands all of a heap; he began to see the dice going against him, and after an obvious hesitation he also hauled himself heavily into the shrouds and, with the dirk in his teeth, began slowly and painfully to mount. It cost him no end of time and groans to haul his wounded leg behind him; and I had finished my arrangements before he was much more than a third of the way up. Then, with a pistol in either hand, I addressed him.

"One more step, Mr. Hands, and I'll blow your brains out!"

He stopped instantly. I could see by the working of his face that he was trying to think. At last, with a swallow or two, he spoke. In order to speak he had to take the dagger from his mouth, but in all else he remained unmoved.

"Jim," says he, "I reckon I'd have had you but for that there lurch; but I don't have no luck, not I; and I reckon I'll have to strike, which comes hard, you see, for a master mariner, to a ship's younker like you."

I was drinking in his words and smiling away, as conceited as a cock upon a wall, when, all in a breath, back went his right hand over his shoulder. Something sang like an arrow through the air; I felt a blow and then a sharp pang, and there I was pinned by the shoulder to the mast. In the horrid pain and surprise of the moment—I scarce can say it was by my own volition, and I am sure it was without a conscious aim—both my pistols went off, and both escaped out of my hands. They did not fall alone; with a choked cry the coxswain loosed his grasp upon the shrouds and plunged head first into the water.

Owing to the cant of the vessel the masts hung far out over the water, and from my perch on the crosstrees I had nothing below me but the surface of the bay. Hands, who was not so far up, was, in consequence, nearer to the ship, and fell between me and the bulwarks. He rose once to the surface in a lather of foam and blood, and then sank again for good. As the water settled I could see him lying huddled together on the clean, bright sand in the shadow of the vessel's side.

I was no sooner certain of this than I began to feel sick, faint and terrified. Blood was running over my back and chest. The dirk, where it had pinned my shoulder to the mast, seemed to burn like a hot iron; yet it was not so much these real sufferings that distressed me; it was the horror I had of falling from the crosstrees into that still green water, beside the body of the coxswain. I clung with both hands and I shut my eyes as if to cover up the peril. Gradually my pulses quieted down, and I was once more in possession of myself.

It was my first thought to pluck forth the dirk, but my nerve failed me and I desisted with a violent shudder. Oddly enough, that very shudder did the business. The knife, in fact, had held me by a mere pinch of skin, and this the shudder tore away. I was my own master again, and only tacked to the mast by my coat and shirt. These last I broke through with a jerk, and then regained the deck.

I went below and did what I could for my wound; it still bled freely, but it was neither deep nor dangerous, nor did it greatly gall me when I used my arm. Then I looked around me, and as the ship was now, in a sense, my own, I began to think of clearing it from its last passenger—the dead man, O'Brien.

As the habit of tragical adventures had worn off almost all my terror for the dead I took him by the waist as if he had been a sack of bran and, with one good heave, tumbled him overboard. He went in with a sounding plunge; the red cap came off and remained floating on the surface; and as soon as the splash subsided I could see him and Israel lying side by side, wavering with the tremulous movement of the water, the quick fishes steering to and fro over both.

The evening breeze had sprung up, and the cordage had begun to sing softly and the idle sails to rattle to and fro. I began to see a danger to the ship. The jibs I speedily doused and brought tumbling to the deck; but the mainsail was a harder matter. When the schooner canted over, the boom had swung outboard, and the cap of it and a foot or two of sail hung even under water. This made it still more dangerous, yet the strain was so heavy that I half feared to meddle. At last I got my knife and cut the halyards. The peak dropped instantly, a great belly of loose canvas floated upon the water, and that was the extent of what I could accomplish.

By this time the whole anchorage had fallen into shadow. The tide was rapidly fleeting seaward, the schooner settling more and more on her beam ends. Holding the cut hawser, I let myself drop softly overboard. The water scarcely reached my waist; and I waded ashore in great spirits, leaving the *Hispaniola* on her side, with her mainsail trailing wide upon the surface of the bay.

I had nothing nearer my fancy than to get home to the stockade and boast of my achievements. Possibly I might be blamed a bit for my truantry, but the recapture of the *Hispaniola* was a clinching answer, and I hoped that even Captain Smollett would confess I had not lost my time.

So thinking, I set my face for the blockhouse and my companions. I remembered that the most easterly of the rivers which drain into Captain Kidd's anchorage ran from the two-peaked hill upon my left; and I bent my course in that direction that I might pass the stream while it was small. The wood was pretty open, and, keeping along the lower spurs, I had soon turned the corner of that hill, and not long after waded across the watercourse.

By now the night was black; it was all I could do to guide myself even roughly toward my destination. But suddenly a brightness fell about me. I looked up; a pale glimmer of moonbeams had alighted on the summit of the Spy-glass, and soon after I saw something broad and silvery moving low down behind the trees, and knew the moon had risen.

With this to help me, I passed rapidly over what remained of my journey. Yet, as I began to thread the grove that lies before the stockade I was not so thoughtless but that I slacked my pace and went a trifle warily. It would have been a poor end of my adventures to get shot down by my own party in mistake.

The moon was climbing higher and higher; its light began to fall here and there in masses through the more open districts of the wood; and in front of me a glow of a different color appeared among the trees. It was red and hot, and now and again it was a little darkened, as it were the embers of a bonfire smoldering. For the life of me I could not think what it might be.

At last I came right down upon the borders of the clearing. The western end was already steeped in moonshine; the rest, and the blockhouse itself, still lay in a black shadow. On the other side of the house an immense fire had burned itself into clear embers and shed a steady, red reverberation.

I stopped. It had not been our way to build great fires; we were, indeed, by the captain's orders, somewhat niggardly of firewood; and I began to fear that something had gone wrong while I was absent.

I stole round by the eastern end, keeping close in shadow, and, at a convenient place, where the darkness was thickest, crossed the palisade and crawled toward the corner of the house. As I drew nearer my heart was suddenly lightened. It is not a pleasant noise in itself, but just then it was like music to hear my friends snoring together so loud and peaceful in their sleep. The sea cry of the watch, that beautiful "All's well," never fell more reassuringly on my ear.

In the meantime there was no doubt of one thing—they kept an infamous bad watch. If it had been Silver and his lads that were now creeping in on them not a soul would have seen daybreak. That was what it was, thought I, to have the captain wounded.

By this time I had got to the door and stood up. All was dark within, so that I could distinguish nothing by the eye. As for sounds, there was the steady drone of the snorers, and a small occasional noies, a flickering or pecking that I could in no way account for. With my arms before me I walked steadily in. I should lie down in my own place (I thought, with a silent chuckle) and enjoy their faces when they found me in the morning.

My foot struck something hard and yielding—it was a sleeper's leg; and he turned and groaned, but without awaking.

And then, suddenly, a shrill voice broke forth out of the darkness: "Pieces of eight! pieces of eight! pieces of eight!"

Silver's green parrot, Captain Flint! It was she whom I had heard pecking at a piece of bark; it was she, keeping better watch than any human being, who thus announced my arrival.

I had no time to recover. At the sharp tone of the parrot the sleepers awoke and sprang up; and with a mighty oath the voice of Silver cried: "Who goes?"

I turned to run, struck violently against one person, recoiled, and ran full into the arms of a second, who closed upon me and held me tight.

"Bring a torch, Dick," said Silver.

XIII. IN THE ENEMY'S CAMP

THE RED GLARE of the torch showed the worst of my apprehensions realized. The pirates were in possession of the house and stores; there was the cask of cognac, there were the pork and bread, and, what tenfold increased my horror, not a sign of any prisoner. I could only judge that all had perished.

There were six of the buccaneers, all told. Five were on their feet, flushed and swollen, suddenly called out of the first sleep of drunkenness. The sixth had only risen upon his elbow; the bloodstained bandage round his head told that he had recently been wounded, and still more recently dressed. I remembered the man who had been shot and had run back among the woods in the great attack, and doubted not that this was he.

The parrot sat, preening her plumage, on Long John's shoulder. He himself, I thought, looked somewhat paler and more stern than I was used to.

"So," said he, "here's Jim Hawkins, shiver my timbers! Dropped in, like, eh? Well, come, I take that friendly." And thereupon he sat down across the brandy cask and began to fill a pipe. "Give me a loan of the link, Dick," said he; and then, when he had a good light, he added, "And so, Jim"—stopping the tobacco—"here you were, and quite a pleasant surprise for poor old John. I see you were smart when first I set my eyes on you; but this here gets away from me clean, it do."

I made no answer. I stood there with my back against the wall, looking Silver in the face—pluckily enough, I hope, but black despair in my heart. Silver took a whiff or two of his pipe, with great composure, and then ran on again. "Now, you see, Jim, so be as you *are* here, I'll give you a piece of my mind. I've always liked you, I have, for a lad of spirit, and the picter of my own self when I was young and handsome. I always wanted you to jine and take your share, and die a gentleman, and now, my cock, you've got to. Cap'n Smollett's a fine seaman, as I'll own up to any day, but stiff on discipline. 'Dooty is dooty,' says he, and right he is. Just you keep clear of the cap'n. The doctor himself is gone dead again' you—'ungrateful scamp' was what he said; and the short and the long of the whole story is about here: you can't go back to your own lot, for they won't have you; and, without you start a third ship's company all by yourself, you'll have to jine with Cap'n Silver."

So far so good. My friends, then, were still alive.

"I don't say nothing as to your being in our hands," continued Silver, "though there you are, and you may lay to it. If you like the service, well, you'll jine; and if you don't, Jim, why, you're free to answer no—free and welcome, shipmate; and if fairer can be said by mortal seaman, shiver my sides!"

"Am I to answer, then?" I asked, with a tremulous voice. Through all this sneering talk I was made to feel the threat of death that overhung me, and my heart beat painfully in my breast.

"Lad," said Silver, "no one's a-pressing of you. Take your bearings. None of us won't hurry you, mate."

"Well," says I, growing a bit bolder, "if I'm to choose, I declare I have a right to know what's what, and why you're here, and where my friends are."

"Wot's wot?" repeated one of the buccaneers in a deep growl. "Ah, he'd be a lucky one as knowed that!"

"You'll, perhaps, batten down your hatches till you're spoke to, my friend," cried Silver, truculently, to this speaker. And then, in his first gracious tones, he replied to me: "Yesterday morning, Mr. Hawkins," said he, "in the dogwatch down came Dr. Livesey with a flag of truce. Says he, 'Cap'n Silver, you're sold out. Ship's gone.' Well, maybe we'd been taking a glass and a song to help it round. Leastways none of us had looked out. We looked out, and, by thunder! the old ship was gone. I never seen a pack of fools look fishier, and you may lay to that. 'Well,' says the doctor, 'let's bargain.' We bargained, him and I, and here we are: stores, brandy, blockhouse, and the firewood you was thoughtful enough to cut. As for them, they've tramped; I don't know where's they are."

He drew again quietly at his pipe. "And lest you should take it into that head of yours," he went on, "that you was included in the treaty, here's the last word that was said: 'How many are you,' says I, 'to leave?' 'Four,' says he—'four, and one of us wounded. As for that boy, I don't know where he is, confound him,' says he, 'nor I don't much care. We're about sick of him.' These were his words."

"Is that all?" I asked.

"Well, it's all you're to hear, my son," returned Silver.

"And now I am to choose?"

"And now you are to choose, and you may lay to that."

"Well," said I, "I am not such a fool but I know pretty well what I have to look for. I've seen too many die since I fell in with you. But there's a thing or two I have to tell you," I said, and by this time I was quite excited; "and the first is this: here you are in a bad way: ship lost, treasure lost, men lost; your whole business gone to wreck; and if you want to know who did it—it was I! I was in the apple barrel the night we sighted land and I heard you, John, and you, Dick Johnson, and Hands, who is now at the bottom of the sea, and told every word you said before the hour was out. And as for the schooner, it was I who cut her cable, and it was I that killed the men you had aboard her, and it was I who brought her where you'll never see her more. I've had the top of this business from the first; I no more fear you than I fear a fly. Kill me, if you please, or spare me. But one thing I'll say, and no more—if you spare me bygones are bygones, and when you fellows are in court for piracy I'll save you all I can. It is for you to choose. Kill another and do yourselves no good, or spare me and keep a witness to save you from the gallows."

I stopped and, to my wonder, not a man of them moved, but all sat staring at me like so many sheep. And while they were still staring I broke out again:

"And now, Mr. Silver," I said, "I believe you're the best man here, and if things go the worst I'll take it kind of you to let the doctor know the way I took it."

"I'll bear it in mind," said Silver, with an accent so curious that I could not decide whether he were laughing at my request, or had been favorably affected by my courage.

"I'll put one to that," cried the old seaman—Morgan by name—whom I had seen in Long John's public house upon the quays of Bristol. "It was him that knowed Black Dog."

"Well, and see here," added the sea cook. "It was this same boy that faked the chart from Billy Bones. First and last, we've split upon Jim Hawkins!"

"Then here goes!" said Morgan, with an oath. And he sprang up, drawing his knife.

"Avast there!" cried Silver. "Who are you, Tom Morgan? Maybe you thought you was cap'n here, perhaps. Cross me, and you'll go where many a good man's gone before you, first and last, these thirty year back."

Morgan paused, but a hoarse murmur rose from the others.

"Tom's right," said one.

"I stood hazing long enough from one," added another. "I'll be hanged if I'll be hazed by you, John Silver."

"Did any of you gentlemen want to have it out with *me?*" roared Silver, bending forward from his position on the keg, with his pipe glowing in his right hand. "Well, him that wants shall get it: I'm ready. Take a cutlass, him that dares, and I'll see the color of his inside, crutch and all, before that pipe's empty."

Not a man stirred; not a man answered.

"That's your sort, is it?" he added, returning his pipe to his mouth. "Well, p'r'aps you can understand King George's English. I'm cap'n here because I'm the best man by a long sea mile. You won't fight as gentlemen o' fortune should; then, by thunder, you'll obey, and you may lay to it! I like that boy. He's more a man than any pair of rats of you in this here house, and what I say is this: let me see him that'll lay a hand on him—that's what I say, and you may lay to it."

There was a long pause after this. I stood straight up against the wall, my heart still going like a sledgehammer, but with a ray of hope now shining in my bosom. Silver leaned back against the wall, his pipe in the corner of his mouth, as calm as though he had been in church; yet he kept the tail of his eye on his unruly followers. They, on their part, drew together toward the far end of the blockhouse, and the low hiss of their whispering sounded in my ear continuously. One after another they would look up, and the red light of the torch would fall for a second on their nervous faces; but it was not toward me, it was toward Silver that they turned their eyes.

"You seem to have a lot to say," remarked Silver, spitting far into the air. "Pipe up and let me hear it, or lay to."

"Ax your pardon, sir," returned one of the men, "you're pretty free with some of the rules; maybe you'll kindly keep an eye upon the rest. This crew's dissatisfied; this crew has its rights like other crews; I take it we can talk together. I ax your pardon, sir, acknowledging you to be capting at this present; but I claim my right, and steps outside for a council."

And with an elaborate sea salute this fellow, a long, yellow-eyed man of five-and-thirty, disappeared out of the house. One after another the rest followed, each making a salute as he passed, each adding some apology. "According to rules," said one. "Fo'c'sle council," said Morgan. And so all marched out and left Silver and me alone.

The sea cook instantly removed his pipe. "Now, look you here, Jim," he said, in a whisper, "you're within half a plank of death and, what's a long sight worse, of torture. They're going to throw me off. But, you mark, I stand by you through thick and thin. I didn't mean to; no, not till you spoke up. I was about desperate to lose that much blunt, and be hanged into the bargain. But I see you was the right sort. I says to myself: You stand by Hawkins, John, and Hawkins'll stand by you. You're his last card, and, by the living thunder, John, he's yours! You save your witness, says I, and he'll save your neck!"

I began to understand. "You mean all's lost?" I asked.

"Aye, by gum, I do!" he answered. "Ship gone, neck gone—that's the size of it. Once I looked into that bay, Jim Hawkins, and seen no schooner—well, I'm tough, but I gave out. As for that lot and their council, mark me, they're outright fools and cowards. I'll save your life—if so be as I can—from them. But, see here, Jim—tit for tat—you save Long John from swinging."

I was bewildered; it seemed a thing so hopeless he was asking—he, the old buccaneer, the ringleader throughout.

"What I can do, that I'll do," I said.

"It's a bargain!" cried Long John.

He hobbled to the torch, where it stood propped among the firewood, and took a fresh light to his pipe. "Understand me, Jim," he said, returning. "I've a head on my shoulders, I have. I'm on Squire's side now. I know you've got that ship safe somewheres. How you done it I don't know, but safe it is. I guess Hands and O'Brien turned soft. Now you mark me. I ask no questions, nor I won't let others. I know when a game's up, I do; and I know a lad that's staunch. Ah, you that's young—you and me might have done a power of good together!"

He drew some cognac from the cask into a tin pannikin. "Will you taste, messmate?" he asked; and when I had refused: "Well, I'll take a drain myself, Jim," said he. "I need a caulker, for there's trouble on hand. And, talking o' trouble, why did that doctor give me the chart, Jim?"

My face expressed a wonder so unaffected that he saw the need-lessness of further questioning. And he took another swallow of the brandy, shaking his great fair head like a man who looks forward to the worst.

XIV. THE BLACK SPOT AGAIN

THE COUNCIL of the buccaneers had lasted some time when one of them re-entered the house and begged for a moment's loan of the torch. Silver agreed; and this emissary retired again, leaving us together in the dark. "There's a breeze coming, Jim," said Silver, who had by this time adopted quite a friendly and familiar tone.

I turned to the loophole nearest me and looked out. The embers of the great fire had so far burned themselves out that I understood why these conspirators desired a torch. About halfway down the slope to the stockade they were collected in a group; one held the light, another was on his knees in their midst, and I saw the blade of an open knife in his hand in the moon and torchlight. The rest were all somewhat stooping, as though watching the maneuvers of this last. I could just make out that he had a book as well as a knife in his hand, and was still wondering how anything so incongruous had come in their possession, when the kneeling figure rose once more to his feet and the whole party began to move together toward the house.

"Here they come," said I.

"Well, let 'em come, lad—let 'em come," said Silver, cheerily. "I've still a shot in my locker."

The door opened and the five men, standing huddled together just inside, pushed one of their number forward, his closed right hand in front of him.

"Step up, lad," cried Silver. "I won't eat you. Hand it over, lubber. I know the rules, I do; I won't hurt a depytation."

Thus encouraged, the buccaneer stepped forth and, having passed something to Silver, slipped back to his companions.

The sea cook looked at what had been given him. "The black spot! I thought so," he observed. "Where might you have got the paper? Why, hillo! look here, now; this ain't lucky! You've gone and cut this out of a Bible. What fool's cut a Bible?"

"Ah, there!" said Morgan. "There! Wot did I say? No good'll come o' that, I said."

"Well, you've about fixed it now among you," continued Silver. "You'll all swing now, I reckon. What softheaded lubber had a Bible?"

"It was Dick," said one.

"Dick, was it? Then Dick can get to prayers," said Silver.

But here the long man with the yellow eyes struck in. "Belay that talk, John Silver," he said. "This crew has tipped you the black spot in full council, as in dooty bound; just you turn it over, as in dooty bound, and see what's wrote there. Then you can talk."

"Thanky, George," replied the sea cook. "You always was brisk for business, and has the rules by heart. Well, what is it, anyway? Ah! 'Deposed'—that's it, is it? Very pretty wrote, to be sure; like print, I swear. Your hand o' write, George? Why, you was gettin' quite a leadin' man in this here crew. You'll be cap'n next, I shouldn't wonder. Just oblige me with that torch again, will you? This pipe don't draw."

"Come now," said George, "you don't fool us no more. You're over now, and you'll maybe step off that barrel and help vote."

"I thought you knowed the rules," returned Silver, contemptuously. "Leastways, if you don't, I do; and I wait here—and I'm still your cap'n, mind—till you outs your grievances and I reply; in the meantime your black spot ain't worth a biscuit."

"Oh," replied George, "you don't be under no kind of apprehension; *we're* all square, we are. First, you've made a hash of this cruise—you'll be a bold man to say no to that. Second, you let the enemy out o' this here trap for nothing. Third, you wouldn't let us go at them upon the march. Oh, we see through you, John Silver; you want to play booty. And fourth, there's this here boy."

"Is that all?" asked Silver, quietly.

"Enough, too," retorted George. "We'll all swing and sun-dry for your bungling."

"Well, I'll answer these four p'ints; one after another I'll answer 'em. You say this cruise is bungled. Ah! if you could understand how bad it's bungled you would see! We're that near the gibbet that my neck's stiff with thinking on it. Well, now, you all know what I wanted; and you all know if that had been done we'd 'a' been aboard the *Hispaniola* this night, every man of us alive, and full of good plum duff, and the treasure in the hold of her, by thunder! Well, who crossed me? Who forced my hand, as was the lawful cap'n? Why, it was Anderson and Hands and you, George Merry! And you have the Davy Jones's insolence to up and stand for cap'n over me—you that sank the lot of us!"

Silver paused, and I could see by the faces of George and his comrades that these words had not been said in vain.

"Go on, John," said Morgan. "Speak up to the others."

"Ah, the others!" returned John. "If you want to know about number four and that boy, why, shiver my timbers! isn't he a hostage? Are we a-going to waste a hostage? No, not us; he might be our last chance, and I shouldn't wonder. Kill that boy? Not me, mates! And number three? Ah, well, there's a deal to say to number three. Maybe you don't count it nothing to have a real college doctor come to see you every day—you, John, with your head broke, or you, George Merry, that had the ague shakes upon you not six hours agone, and has your eyes the color of lemon peel to this same moment on the clock? And maybe, perhaps, you didn't know there was a consort coming, either? But there is, and not so long till then; and we'll see who'll be glad to have a hostage when it comes to that. And as for number two, and why I made a bargain—well, you'd have starved if I hadn't— But that's a trifle! You look there—that's why!"

And he cast down upon the floor a paper that I instantly recognized—none other than the chart with the three red crosses that I had found at the bottom of the captain's chest. Why the doctor had given it to him was more than I could fancy.

But if it were inexplicable to me, the appearance of the chart was incredible to the surviving mutineers. They leaped upon it like cats upon a mouse. It went from hand to hand; and by the oaths and the cries and the childish laughter you would have thought, not only they were fingering the very gold, but were at sea with it, besides, in safety.

"Yes," said one, "that's Flint, sure enough. J. F., and a score below with a clove hitch to it; so he done ever."

"Mighty pretty," said George. "But how are we to get away with it, and us no ship?"

Silver sprang up and, supporting himself with a hand against the wall, "Now I give you warning, George," he cried. "One more word of your sauce and I'll call you down and fight you. How? Why, how do I know? You had ought to tell me that—you and the rest that lost me my schooner with your interference, burn you! But not you; you hain't got the invention of a cockroach. But civil you can speak, and shall, George Merry."

"That's fair enow," said the old man Morgan.

"Fair! I reckon so," said the sea cook. "You lost the ship; I found the treasure. Who's the better man at that? And now I resign, by thunder! Elect whom you please to be your cap'n. I'm done with it."

"Silver!" they cried. "Barbecue for ever! Barbecue for cap'n!"

"So that's the toon, is it?" cried the cook. "George, I reckon you'll have to wait another turn, friend. And now, shipmates, this black spot? 'Tain't much good now, is it? Dick's crossed his luck and spoiled his Bible, and that's about all. Here, Jim—here's a cur'osity for you," he added and tossed me the paper.

It was a round about the size of a crown piece. One side was blank, for it had been the last leaf; the other contained a verse or two of Revelation—these words among the rest: *Without are dogs . . . and murderers*. The printed side had been blackened with wood ash, which already began to come off; on the blank side had been written with the same material the one word "Deposed." I have that curiosity beside me at this moment, but not a trace of writing now remains.

That was the end of the night's business. Soon after we lay down to sleep. It was long ere I could close an eye, and Heaven knows I had matter enough for thought in the man whom I had slain that afternoon, in my own most perilous position, and in the remarkable game that I saw Silver now engaged upon—keeping the mutineers together with one hand, and grasping with the other after every means to make his peace and save his miserable life.

I WAS WAKENED—indeed, we were all wakened—by a clear, hearty voice hailing us from the margin of the wood: "Blockhouse, ahoy!" it cried. "Here's the doctor."

And the doctor it was. Although I was glad to hear the sound, yet my gladness was not without admixture. I remembered my insubordinate and stealthy conduct; and when I saw where it had brought me I felt ashamed to look him in the face.

"Top o' the morning to you, sir!" cried Silver, broad awake and beaming with good nature in a moment. "George, shake up your timbers, and help Dr. Livesey over the ship's side. All a-doin' well, your patients was—and all well and merry." So he pattered on, standing on the hilltop with his crutch—quite the old John in voice, manner, and expression.

"We've quite a surprise for you, too, sir," he continued. "We've a little stranger here—he! he! A noo boarder and lodger."

Dr. Livesey was by this time across the stockade, and I could hear the alteration in his voice as he said: "Not Jim?"

"The very same Jim as ever was," says Silver.

The doctor stopped outright, and it was some seconds before he seemed able to move on. "Well, well," he said at last, "duty first and pleasure afterward, as you might have said yourself, Silver. Let us overhaul these patients of yours."

He entered the blockhouse and, with a grim nod to me, proceeded with his work among the sick. He seemed under no apprehension, though he must have known that his life, among these treacherous demons, depended on a hair; and he rattled on to his patients as if he were paying an ordinary professional visit in a quiet English family.

"You're doing well, my friend," he said to the fellow with the bandaged head; "and if ever any person had a close shave, it was you; your head must be as hard as iron. Well, George, how goes it? You're a pretty color, certainly; why, your liver, man, is upside down! Did he take that medicine, men?"

"Ay, ay, sir, he took it, sure enough," returned Morgan.

"Because, you see, since I am mutineers' doctor, or prison doctor, as I prefer to call it," says Dr. Livesey, in his pleasantest way, "I make it a point of honor not to lose a man for King George (God bless him!) and the gallows."

The rogues looked at each other, but swallowed the home thrust in silence.

"Dick don't feel well, sir," said one.

"Don't he?" replied the doctor. "Well, step up here, Dick, and let me see your tongue. No, I should be surprised if he did! The man's tongue is fit to frighten the French. Another fever."

"Ah, there," said Morgan, "that comed of sp'iling Bibles."

"That comed—as you call it—of being arrant asses," retorted the doctor, "and not having sense enough to know honest air from poison, and the dry land from a vile, pestiferous slough. I think it probable—though it's only an opinion—that you'll all have the deuce to pay before you get that malaria out of your systems. Camp in a bog, would you? Silver, I'm surprised at you. You're less of a fool than many, but you don't appear to me to have a notion of the rules of health.

"Well," he added, after he had dosed them round—"that's done for today. And now I should wish to have a talk with that boy, please." And he nodded in my direction carelessly.

George Merry was at the door, spluttering over some bad-tasting medicine, but at the doctor's proposal he swung round and cried, "No," and swore.

Silver struck the barrel with his open hand. "Si-lence!" he roared, and looked about him positively like a lion. "Doctor," he went on in his usual tones, "I was a-thinking of that, knowing as how you had a fancy for the boy. We're all humbly grateful for your kindness and, as you see, puts faith in you, and takes the drugs down like that much grog. And I've found a way as'll suit all. Hawkins, will you give me your word of honor as a young gentleman—for a young gentleman you are, although poor born—not to slip your cable?"

I readily gave the pledge required.

"Then, Doctor," said Silver, "you just step outside o' that stockade, and once you're there I'll bring the boy down on the inside, and I reckon you can yarn through the spars."

The explosion of disapproval broke out immediately the doctor had left the house. Silver was roundly accused of playing double—of trying to make a separate peace for himself—in one word, of the identical thing that he was doing. But he called them all fools and dolts, said it was necessary I should talk to the doctor, fluttered the chart in their faces, and asked them if they could afford to break the treaty the very day they were bound a-treasure-hunting.

"No, by thunder!" he cried. "It's us must break the treaty when the time's come, and till then I'll gammon that doctor if I have to ile his boots with brandy." Then he stalked out upon his crutch, with his hand on my shoulder, leaving them silenced by his volubility rather than convinced. "Slow, lad, slow," he said. "They might round upon us in a twinkle of an eye if we was seen to hurry."

Very deliberately, then, did we advance across the sand to where the doctor awaited us on the other side of the stockade, and as soon as we were within easy speaking distance Silver stopped.

"You'll make a note of this here also, Doctor," says he, "and the boy'll tell you how I saved his life and were deposed for it, too, and you may lay to that. Doctor, when a man's steering as near the wind as me you wouldn't think it too much, mayhap, to give him one good word? You'll bear in mind it's not my life only now—it's that boy's into the bargain; and you'll speak me fair, Doctor, and give me a bit o' hope to go on, for the sake of mercy." Silver was a changed man once he had his back to his friends and the blockhouse; his voice trembled; never was a soul more dead in earnest.

"Why, John, you're not afraid?" asked Dr. Livesey.

"Doctor, I'm no coward! No, not I—not so much!" and he snapped his fingers. "But I'll own up fairly, I've the shakes upon me for the gallows. You're a good man and a true. And you'll not forget what I done good, not any more than you'll forget the bad, I know. And I step aside—and leave you and Jim alone. And you'll put that down for me, too." So saying, he stepped back till he was out of earshot, and there sat down on a stump and began to whistle.

"So, Jim," said the doctor, sadly, "here you are. Heaven knows I cannot find it in my heart to blame you, but this much I will say: when Captain Smollett was well you dared not have gone off, and when he was ill and couldn't help it, by George, it was downright cowardly!"

I will own that I here began to weep. "Doctor," I said, "you might spare me. I have blamed myself enough; my life's forfeit anyway, and I should have been dead by now if Silver hadn't stood for me; and, Doctor, believe this, I can die, but if they come to torture me—"

"Jim," the doctor interrupted, and his voice was quite changed—"I can't have this. Whip over and we'll run for it."

"Doctor," said I, "I passed my word."

"I know, I know," he cried. "I'll take it on my shoulders, but stay here I cannot let you. Jump! One jump and you're out, and we'll run for it like antelopes."

"No," I replied, "you know right well you wouldn't do the thing yourself; neither you nor Squire nor Captain, and no more will I. But, Doctor, you did not let me finish. If they come to torture me I might let slip a word of where the ship is, for I got the ship, part by luck and part by risking, and she lies in North Inlet, on the southern beach, and just below high water."

"The ship!" exclaimed the doctor.

Rapidly I described to him my adventures, and he heard me out in silence.

"There is a kind of fate in this," he observed, when I had done. "Every step it's you that saves our lives. You found out the plot; you found Ben Gunn—the best deed that ever you did or will do, though you live to ninety. Oh, by Jupiter! and talking of Ben Gunn, why, this is the mischief in person. Silver!" he cried, "Silver!—I'll give you a piece of advice," he continued as the cook drew near again; "don't you be in any great hurry after that treasure."

"Why, sir," said Silver, "I can only save my life and the boy's by seeking for that treasure; and you may lay to that."

"Well, Silver," replied the doctor, "if that is so I'll go one step further; look out for squalls when you find it."

"Sir," said Silver, "that's too much and too little. Why you left the blockhouse, why you given me that there chart, I don't know. And yet I done your bidding with never a word of hope! But this here's too much. If you won't tell me what you mean plain out, just say so, and I'll leave the helm."

"No," said the doctor, "I've no right to say more; it's not my secret. But I'll give you a bit of hope; Silver, if we both get alive out of this wolf trap I'll do my best to save you, short of perjury."

Silver's face was radiant. "You couldn't say more, sir, not if you was my mother," he cried.

"Well, that's my first concession," added the doctor. "My second is a piece of advice: Keep the boy close beside you, and when you need help, halloo. I'm off to seek it for you. Good-by, Jim."

And Dr. Livesey shook hands with me through the stockade and set off at a brisk pace into the wood.

XV. THE TREASURE HUNT—FLINT'S POINTER

"Jim," said Silver, when we were alone, "if I saved your life, you saved mine. I seen the doctor waving you to run for it—with the tail of my eye, I did; and I seen you say no, as plain as hearing. Jim, that's one to you. This is the first glint of hope I had since the attack failed, and I owe it to you. And now, Jim, we're to go in for this here treasure-hunting; and you and me must stick close and we'll save our necks in spite o' fate and fortune."

Just then a man hailed us from the fire that breakfast was ready, and we were soon seated about the sand over biscuit and fried junk.

"Ay, mates," said Silver, eating away, with Captain Flint on his shoulder, "it's lucky you have Barbecue to think for you. I got what I wanted, I did. Sure enough, they have the ship. Where they have it I don't know yet; but once we hit the treasure, we'll have to jump about and find out. And then, mates, us that has the boats, I reckon, has the upper hand."

Thus he kept running on, with his mouth full of the hot bacon: thus he restored their hope and confidence, and, I suspect, repaired his own at the same time. "As for hostage," he continued, "that's his last talk, I guess, with them he loves so dear. I've got my piece o' news, and thanky to him for that, but it's over and done. I'll take him in a line when we go treasure-hunting, for we'll keep him like so much gold, in case of accidents, you mark. Once we got the ship and treasure both, and off to sea, why then we'll talk Mr. Hawkins over, we will, and we'll give him his share, to be sure, for all his kindness."

It was no wonder the men were in a good humor now. For my part, I was horribly cast down. Should the scheme he had now sketched prove feasible, Silver, already doubly a traitor, would not hesitate to adopt it. He had still a foot in either camp, and there was no doubt he would prefer wealth and freedom with the pirates to a bare escape from hanging, which was the best he had to hope on our side.

Nay, and even if things so fell out that he was forced to keep his faith with Dr. Livesey, even then what danger lay before us! What a moment that would be when the suspicions of his followers turned to certainty and he and I should have to fight for dear life against five active seamen!

Add to this the mystery that still hung over the behavior of my friends, their unexplained desertion of the stockade, their inexplicable cession of the chart, or harder still to understand, the doctor's last warning to Silver, "Look out for squalls when you find it," and you will readily believe with how uneasy a heart I set forth behind my captors on the quest for treasure.

We made a curious figure, all in soiled sailor clothes and all but me armed to the teeth. Silver had two guns slung about him—one before and one behind—besides the great cutlass at his waist and a pistol in each pocket of his square-tailed coat. To complete his strange appearance Captain Flint sat perched upon his shoulder and gabbling odds and ends of purposeless sea talk. I had a line to my waist, and followed obediently after the sea cook, who held the loose end of the rope. For all the world, I was led like a dancing bear.

The other men were variously burthened, some carrying picks and shovels—for that had been the very first necessary they brought ashore from the *Hispaniola*—others laden with pork, bread, and brandy for the midday meal. All the stores, I observed, came from our stock; and I could see the truth of Silver's words the night before. Had he not struck a bargain with the doctor, he and his mutineers must have been driven to subsist on water and the proceeds of their hunting.

Well, thus equipped, we all set out—even the fellow with the broken head—and straggled to the beach, where the two gigs awaited us. With our numbers divided between them, we set forth upon the bosom of the anchorage. As we pulled there was some discussion on the chart. The red cross was, of course, far too large to be a guide; and the terms of the note on the back admitted to some ambiguity. They ran, the reader may remember, thus:

Tall tree, Spye-glass shoulder, bearing a point to the N. of N.N.E.
Skeleton Island E.S.E. and by E.
Ten feet.

A tall tree was thus the principal mark. Now, right before us, the anchorage was bounded by a plateau from two to three hundred feet high, adjoining on the north the sloping southern shoulder of the Spy-glass. The top of the plateau was dotted with pine trees of varying height. Every here and there one of a different species rose forty or fifty feet clear above its neighbors, and which of these was the particular "tall tree" of Captain Flint could only be decided on the spot and by the readings of the compass.

We pulled easily, by Silver's directions, and landed at the mouth of the second river—that which runs down a woody cleft of the Spyglass. Thence we began to ascend the slope toward the plateau. At the outset miry ground and matted vegetation delayed our progress; but by little and little the hill began to steepen and the wood to change its character and to grow more open. It was, indeed, a most pleasant portion of the island that we were now approaching.

The party spread itself abroad, shouting and leaping to and fro. Silver and I followed—I tethered by my rope, he plowing, with deep pants, among the sliding gravel. From time to time, indeed, I had to lend him a hand or he must have missed his footing. We had thus proceeded for about half a mile when the man upon the farthest left began to cry aloud, as if in terror. The others began to run in his direction.

"He can't 'a' found the treasure," said Old Morgan, hurrying past us, "for that's clean atop."

Indeed, as we found when we also reached the spot, it was something very different. At the foot of a pretty big pine, and involved in a green creeper, a human skeleton lay, with a few shreds of clothing, on the ground. I believe a chill struck for a moment to every heart.

"He was a seaman," said George Merry, who was examining the rags of clothing. "Leastways, this is good sea cloth."

"Ay, ay," said Silver, "like enough; you wouldn't look to find a bishop here, I reckon. But what sort of a way is that for bones to lie? 'Tain't in natur'."

Indeed, it seemed impossible to fancy that the body was in a natural position. But for some disarray (the work, perhaps, of the birds that had fed upon him or of the slow-growing creeper that had gradually enveloped his remains) the man lay perfectly straight—his feet pointing in one direction, his hands, raised above his head like a diver's, pointing in the opposite.

"I've taken a notion into my old numskull," observed Silver. "Here's the compass; there's the tip-top p'int o' Skeleton Island, stickin' out like a tooth. Just take a bearing, will you, along the line of them bones."

It was done. The body pointed straight in the direction of the island, and the compass read duly E. S. E. and by E.

"I thought so," cried the cook; "this here is a p'inter. Right up there is our line for the Pole Star and the jolly dollars. But, by thunder! if it don't make me cold inside to think of Flint. This is one of *his* jokes, and no mistake. Him and these six was alone here; he killed 'em, every man; and this one he hauled here and laid down by compass, shiver my timbers! They're long bones, and the hair's been yellow. Ay, that would be Allardyce. You mind Allardyce, Tom Morgan?"

"Ay, ay," returned Morgan, "I mind him; he owed me money, he did, and took my knife ashore with him."

"Great guns! messmates," cried Silver, "but if Flint was living this would be a hot spot for you and me. Six they were, and six are we; and bones is what they are now."

"I saw him dead with these here deadlights," said Morgan. "Billy took me in. There he laid, with penny pieces on his eyes."

"Dead—ay, and gone below," said the man with the bandage; "but if ever sperrit walked, it would be Flint's. Dear heart, but he died bad!"

"Ay, that he did," observed another; "now he raged, and now he hollered for the rum, and now he sang. 'Fifteen Men' were his only song, mates; and I tell you true I never rightly liked to hear it since."

"Come, come," said Silver, "stow this talk. He's dead, and he don't walk—leastways, not by day. Fetch ahead for the doubloons."

We started, but the pirates now kept side by side and spoke with bated breath. The terror of the dead buccaneer had fallen on their spirits.

Partly from the damping influence of this alarm, partly to rest Silver and the sick folk, the whole party sat down as soon as they had gained the brow of the ascent. Sheer above us rose the Spy-glass. There was no sound but that of the distant breakers, mounting from all round. Silver, as he sat, took certain bearings with his compass.

"There are three 'tall trees,'" said he, "about in the right line from Skeleton Island. 'Spye-glass shoulder,' I take it, means that lower p'int there. It's child's play to find the stuff now. I've half a mind to dine first."

"I don't feel sharp," growled Morgan. "Thinkin' o' Flint—I think it were—has done me."

"Ah, well, my son, you praise your stars he's dead," said Silver.

"He were an ugly devil," cried a third pirate, with a shudder; "that blue in the face, too!"

"That was how the rum took him," added Merry.

Ever since they had found the skeleton and got upon this train of thought they had spoken lower and lower, almost to whispering, so that the sound of their talk hardly interrupted the silence of the wood. All of a sudden, out of the middle of the trees in front of us, a high, trembling voice struck up the well-known air and words:

> *"Fifteen men on the Dead Man's Chest—*
> *Yo-ho-ho, and a bottle of rum!"*

I never have seen men more dreadfully affected than the pirates. The color went from their faces; some leaped to their feet, some clawed hold of others.

"It's Flint, by—!" cried Merry.

The song had broken off suddenly—as though someone had laid his hand upon the singer's mouth. Coming through the clear, sunny atmosphere among the green treetops, I thought it had sounded airily and sweetly; and the effect on my companions was the stranger.

"Come," said Silver, struggling with ashen lips to get the word out, "this won't do. I can't name the voice, but it's someone skylarking—someone that's flesh and blood, and you may lay to that."

Already the others had begun to lend an ear to this encouragement when the same voice broke out again—not this time singing, but in a faint distant hail that echoed yet fainter among the clefts of the Spy-glass. "Darby M'Graw!" it wailed—for that is the word that best describes the sound—"Darby M'Graw! Darby M'Graw!" again and again and again; and then rising a little higher, and with an oath that I leave out, "Fetch aft the rum, Darby!"

The buccaneers remained rooted to the ground, their eyes starting from their heads.

"That fixes it!" gasped one. "Let's go."

"They were his last words," moaned Morgan, "his last words aboveboard."

I could hear Silver's teeth rattle in his head, but he had not yet surrendered. "Nobody in this here island ever heard of Darby," he muttered, "not one but us that's here." And then, making a great effort, "Shipmates," he cried, "I never was feared of Flint in his life, and, by the powers, I'll face him dead. There's seven hundred thousand pound not a quarter of a mile from here. When did ever a gentleman o' fortune show his stern to that much dollars for a boozy old seaman with a blue mug—and him dead, too?"

"Belay there, John!" said Merry. "Don't you cross a sperrit."

And the rest were all too terrified to reply. They would have run away severally had they dared, but fear kept them together, and kept them close by John, as if his daring helped them. He, on his part, had pretty well fought his weakness down.

"Sperrit? Well, maybe," he said. "But there's one thing not clear to me. There was an echo. Now, no man ever seen a sperrit with a shadow; well, then, what's he doing with an echo, I should like to know? That ain't in natur', surely?"

This argument seemed weak enough to me. But you can never tell what will affect the superstitious, and, to my wonder, George Merry was greatly relieved. "Well, that's so," he said. "You've a head upon your shoulders, John, and no mistake. 'Bout ship, mates! this here crew is on a wrong tack, I do believe. And come to think of it, it was like Flint's voice, I grant you, but not just so clear away like it, after all. It was liker somebody else's voice now—it was liker—"

"By the powers, Ben Gunn!" roared Silver.

"Ay, and so it were," cried Morgan. "Ben Gunn it were!"

"It don't make much odds, do it now?" asked Dick. "Ben Gunn's not here in the body, any more'n Flint."

But the older hands greeted this remark with scorn.

"Why, nobody minds Ben Gunn," cried Merry, "dead or alive, nobody minds him."

It was extraordinary how their spirits had returned. Soon, hearing no further sound, they shouldered the tools and set forth again, Merry walking first with Silver's compass to keep them on the right line with Skeleton Island. He had said the truth: dead or alive, nobody minded Ben Gunn.

It was fine open walking here, for the pines, great and small, grew wide apart, and between the clumps of nutmeg and azalea, open spaces baked in the hot sunshine. Striking northwest across the island, we drew, on the one hand, ever nearer under the shoulders of the Spyglass, and, on the other, looked ever wider over that western bay where I had once tossed and trembled in the coracle.

The first of the tall trees was reached, and by the bearing proved the wrong one. So with the second. The third rose nearly two hundred feet in the air above a clump of underwood, a giant red column as big as a cottage. It was conspicuous far to sea both on the east and west, and might have been entered as a sailing mark upon the chart.

But it was not its size that now impressed my companions; it was the knowledge that seven hundred thousand pounds in gold lay somewhere buried beneath its spreading shadow. Their eyes burned; their whole soul was bound up in that fortune, that whole lifetime of extravagance and pleasure that lay waiting there for each of them.

Silver hobbled, grunting, on his crutch; his nostrils quivered; he plucked furiously at the line that held me to him, and, from time to time, turned his eyes upon me with a deadly look. Certainly he took no pains to hide his thoughts; and certainly I read them like print. In the immediate nearness of the gold all else had been forgotten; his promise and the doctor's warning were things of the past; and I could not doubt that he hoped to seize upon the treasure, find and board the *Hispaniola* under cover of night, cut every honest throat about that island, and sail away, laden with crimes and riches.

Shaken as I was with those alarms, it was hard for me to keep up with the rapid pace of the treasure hunters. Now and again I stumbled; and it was then that Silver plucked so roughly at the rope and launched at me his murderous glances.

We were now at the margin of the thicket. "Huzza, mates, all together!" shouted Merry; and the foremost broke into a run.

Suddenly we beheld them stop. A low cry arose. Silver doubled his pace, digging away with the foot of his crutch like one possessed; and next moment he and I had also come to a dead halt.

Before us was a great excavation, not very recent, for grass had sprouted on the bottom. In this were the shaft of a pick broken in two and the boards of several packing cases strewn around. On one of these boards I saw, branded with a hot iron, the name *Walrus*—the name of Flint's ship.

The cache had been found and rifled; the seven hundred thousand pounds were gone!

XVI. THE FALL OF A CHIEFTAIN

Each of these six men was as though he had been struck. But with Silver the blow passed almost instantly. Every thought of his soul had been set full-stretch, like a racer, on that money; well, he was brought up in a single second, dead; and he kept his head and changed his plan before the others had had time to realize the disappointment.

"Jim," he whispered, "take that, and stand by for trouble."

And he passed me a double-barreled pistol, and dropped the line that bound me to him. At the same time he began quietly moving, and in a few steps had put the hollow between us two and the other five. Then he looked at me and nodded, as much as to say, "Here is a narrow corner." His looks were now quite friendly; and I was so revolted at these constant changes that I could not forbear whispering, "So you've changed sides again."

There was no time left for him to answer in. The buccaneers, with oaths and cries, began to leap into the pit and to dig with their fingers, throwing the boards aside as they did so. Morgan found a piece of gold. He held it up with a perfect spout of oaths. It was a two-guinea piece, and it went from hand to hand among them.

"Two guineas!" roared Merry, shaking it at Silver. "That's your seven hundred thousand pounds, is it? You're the man for bargains, ain't you? You're him that never bungled nothing, you wooden-headed lubber!"

"Ah, Merry," remarked Silver, "standing for cap'n again? You're a pushing lad, to be sure."

But this time everyone was in Merry's favor. They began to scramble out of the excavation, darting furious glances behind them. One thing I observed, which looked well for us—they all got out upon the opposite side from Silver.

Well, there we stood, two on one side, five on the other, the pit between us. Silver never moved; he watched them, very upright on his crutch, and looked as cool as ever I saw him. He was brave, and no mistake.

At last, Merry seemed to think a speech might help. "Mates," says he, "there's two of them alone there; one's the old cripple that blundered us down to this; the other's that cub I mean to have the heart of—"

He was raising his arm, and plainly meant to lead a charge. But just then, crack! crack! crack!—three musket shots flashed out of the thicket. Merry tumbled head foremost into the excavation; the man with the bandage spun round and fell upon his side, where he lay dead; and the other three turned and ran for it with all their might.

Before you could wink Silver had fired two barrels of a pistol into the struggling Merry; and as the man rolled his eyes at him in the last agony, "George," said he, "I reckon I settled you."

At the same moment the doctor, Gray, and Ben Gunn joined us, with smoking muskets, from among the nutmeg trees.

"Forward!" cried the doctor. "Double-quick, my lads. We must head 'em off the boats." And we set off at a great pace, sometimes plunging through the bushes to the chest.

I tell you but Silver was anxious to keep up with us. The work that man went through, leaping on his crutch till the muscles of his chest were fit to burst, was work no sound man ever equaled; and so thinks the doctor. As it was, he was thirty yards behind us when we reached the brow of the slope. "Doctor," he hailed, "see there! No hurry!"

Sure enough there was no hurry. Across the plateau we could see the three survivors still running in the same direction as they had started, right for Mizzenmast Hill. We were already between them and the boats; and so we four sat down to breathe, while Long John, mopping his face, came slowly up with us. "Thank ye kindly, Doctor," says he. "You came in about the nick, I guess. And so it's you, Ben Gunn!" he added. "Well, you're a nice one, to be sure."

"I'm Ben Gunn, I am," replied the maroon, wriggling in embarrassment. "How do, Mr. Silver. Pretty well, I thank ye, says you."

"Ben, Ben," murmured Silver, "to think as you've done me!"

The doctor sent back Gray for one of the pickaxes deserted, in their flight, by the mutineers; and then, as we proceeded to where the boats were lying, related what had taken place. It was a story that profoundly interested Silver; and Ben Gunn was the hero from beginning to end. In his lonely wanderings about the island, Ben had found the skeleton; he had found the treasure; he had dug it up (it was the shaft of his pickax that lay in the excavation); he had carried it on his back in many weary journeys to a cave on the two-pointed hill at the northeast angle of the island, and there it had lain stored in safety since two months before the arrival of the *Hispaniola*.

When the doctor had wormed this secret from him on the afternoon of the attack, and when, next morning, he saw the anchorage deserted, he had gone to Silver, given him the chart, which was now useless, given him the stores—for Ben Gunn's cave was well supplied with goats' meat salted by himself—given anything and everything to get a chance of moving in safety from the stockade to the two-pointed hill, there to be clear of malaria and keep a guard upon the money.

"As for you, Jim," he said, "it went against my heart, but I did what I thought best for those who had stood by their duty."

That morning, finding that I was to be involved in the horrid disappointment he had prepared for the mutineers, he had run all the way to the cave and, leaving Squire to guard the captain, had taken Gray and the maroon and started, making the diagonal across the island, to be at hand beside the pine. Soon, however, he saw that our party had the start of him; and Ben Gunn, being fleet of foot, had been despatched in front to do his best alone. Then it had occurred to Ben to work upon the superstitions of his former shipmates; and he was so far successful that Gray and the doctor had come up and were already ambushed before the arrival of the treasure hunters.

"Ah," said Silver, "it was fortunate for me that I had Hawkins here. You would have let old John be cut to bits and never given it a thought."

"Not a thought," replied Dr. Livesey, cheerily.

And by this time we had reached the gigs. The doctor, with the pickax, demolished one of them, and then we all got aboard the other and set out for North Inlet. This was a run of eight or nine miles. Silver, though he was almost killed already with fatigue, was set to an oar, like the rest of us, and we were soon skimming swiftly over a smooth sea. We passed out of the straits and doubled the southeast corner of the island, round which, four days ago, we had towed the *Hispaniola*. As we passed the two-pointed hill we could see the black mouth of Ben Gunn's cave and a figure standing by it, leaning on a musket. It was the squire; and we waved a handkerchief and gave him three cheers in which the voice of Silver joined as heartily as any.

Three miles farther, just inside the mouth of North Inlet, what should we meet but the *Hispaniola*, cruising by herself? The last flood had lifted her, and, had there been much wind or a strong tide current, as in the southern anchorage, we should never have found her more. As it was, there was little amiss beyond the wreck of the mainsail. Another anchor was got ready and dropped in a fathom and a half of water. We all pulled round again to Rum Cove, the nearest point for Ben Gunn's treasure house; and then Gray returned with the gig to the *Hispaniola*, where he was to pass the night on guard.

A gentle slope ran up from the beach to the entrance of the cave. At the top the squire met us. To me he was cordial and kind, saying nothing of my escapade. At Silver's polite salute he somewhat flushed. "John Silver," he said, "you're a prodigious villain and a monstrous impostor. I am told I am not to prosecute you. Well, then I will not. But the dead men, sir, hang about your neck like millstones."

"Thank you kindly, sir," replied Long John, again saluting.

And thereupon we all entered the cave. It was a large, airy place, with a little spring and a pool of clear water. The floor was sand. Before a big fire lay Captain Smollett; and in a far corner, only duskily flickered over by the blaze, I beheld great heaps of coin and quadrilaterals built of bars of gold. That was Flint's treasure that we had come so far to seek and that had cost already the lives of seventeen men from the *Hispaniola*. How many it had cost in the amassing, what blood and sorrow, what good ships scuttled on the deep, what brave men walking the plank, what shame and lies and cruelty, perhaps no man alive could tell. Yet there were still three upon that island—Silver and old Morgan and Ben Gunn—who had each taken his share in these crimes, as each had hoped in vain to share in the reward.

"Come in, Jim," said the captain. "You're a good boy in your line, Jim; but I don't think you and me'll go to sea again. Is that you, John Silver? What brings you here, man?"

"Come back to my dooty, sir," returned Silver.

"Ah!" said the captain, and that was all he said.

What a supper I had of it that night, with all my friends around me; and what a meal it was, with Ben Gunn's salted goat and some delicacies and a bottle of old wine from the *Hispaniola*. Never, I am sure, were people gayer or happier. And there was Silver, sitting back out of the firelight, but prompt to spring forward when anything was wanted—the same bland, polite, obsequious seaman of the voyage out.

XVII. AND LAST

THE NEXT morning we fell early to work, for the transportation of this great mass of gold near a mile by land to the beach, and thence three miles by boat to the *Hispaniola*, was a considerable task. The three fellows still abroad upon the island did not greatly trouble us; a single sentry on the shoulder of the hill was sufficient to insure us against any sudden onslaught.

Therefore the work was pushed on briskly. Gray and Ben Gunn came and went with the boat, while the rest, during their absences, piled treasure on the beach. Two of the bars, slung in a rope's end, made a good load for a grown man. For my part, I was kept busy all day in the cave, packing the minted money into bread bags.

It was a strange collection, like Billy Bones's hoard for the diversity of coinage, but so much larger and so much more varied that I think I never had more pleasure than in sorting them. English, French, Spanish, Portuguese, Georges and louis, doubloons and double guineas and moidores and sequins, the pictures of all the kings of Europe for the last hundred years, strange Oriental pieces, round pieces and square pieces, and pieces bored through the middle, as if to wear them round your neck—nearly every variety of money in the world must, I think, have found a place in that collection.

Day after day this work went on; by every evening a fortune had been stowed aboard, but there was another fortune waiting for the morrow; and all this time we saw nothing of the three surviving mutineers. Only once we heard a gunshot a great way off, and supposed them to be hunting. A council was held, and it was decided that we must desert them on the island—to the huge glee, I must say, of Ben Gunn, and with the strong approval of Gray. We left a good stock of powder and shot, the bulk of the salt goat, a few medicines, and some other necessaries, and, by the particular desire of the doctor, a handsome present of tobacco.

That was about our last doing on the island. Before that, we had already got the treasure stowed, and had shipped enough water and the remainder of the goat meat; and at last, one fine morning, we weighed anchor and stood out of North Inlet, the same colors flying that the captain had fought under at the palisade.

The three fellows must have been watching us closer than we thought. For, coming through the narrows, we had to lie very near the southern point, and there we saw all three of them kneeling together on a spit of sand, with their arms raised in supplication. It went to our hearts, I think, to leave them in that wretched state, but we could not risk another mutiny; and to take them home for the gibbet would have been a cruel sort of kindness. The doctor hailed them and told them of the stores we had left, and where they were to find them. But they continued to call us by name and appeal to us, for God's sake, to be merciful and not leave them to die in such a place.

At last, seeing the ship still bore on her course, one of them leaped to his feet, whipped his musket to his shoulder and sent a shot whistling through the mainsail.

After that we kept under cover of the bulwarks, and when next I looked out they had disappeared from the spit and the spit itself had almost melted out of sight. And before noon, to my inexpressible joy, the highest rock of Treasure Island had sunk into the blue round of sea.

We were so short of men that everyone on board had to bear a hand—only the captain lying on a mattress in the stern and giving his orders; for, though greatly recovered, he was still in want of quiet. We laid her head for the nearest port in Spanish America, for we could not risk the voyage home without fresh hands.

It was just at sundown when we cast anchor in a most beautiful landlocked gulf, and were immediately surrounded by shore boats full of Negroes and Mexican Indians and half bloods, selling fruits and vegetables and offering to dive for bits of money. The sight of so many good-humored faces, the taste of the tropical fruits, and, above all, the lights that began to shine in the town, made a most charming contrast to our dark and bloody sojourn on the island; and the doctor and the squire, taking me along with them, went ashore to pass the early part of the night. Here they fell in talk with the captain of an English man-of-war, went on board his ship, and, in short, had so agreeable a time that day was breaking when we came alongside the *Hispaniola*.

As soon as we came on board, Ben Gunn began, with wonderful contortions, to make us a confession. Silver was gone. The maroon had connived at his escape in a shore boat some hours ago, and he now assured us he had only done so to preserve our lives, which would certainly have been forfeit if "that man with the one leg had stayed aboard." But the sea cook had not gone empty-handed. He had cut through a bulkhead unobserved, and had removed one of the sacks of coin, worth, perhaps, three or four hundred guineas, to help him on his further wanderings.

I think we were all pleased to be so cheaply quit of him.

Well, to make a long story short, we got a few hands on board, made a good cruise home, and the *Hispaniola* reached Bristol just as Mr. Blandly was beginning to think of fitting out her consort. Five men only of those who had sailed returned with her. "Drink and the devil had done for the rest," with a vengeance.

All of us had an ample share of the treasure, and used it wisely or foolishly, according to our natures. Captain Smollett is now retired from the sea. Gray not only saved his money, but being suddenly smit with a desire to rise, also studied his profession, and he is now mate and part owner of a fine full-rigged ship. As for Ben Gunn, he got a thousand pounds, which he spent or lost in three weeks, or, to be more exact, in nineteen days, for he was back begging on the twentieth. Then he was given a lodge to keep, exactly as he had feared upon the island.

Of Silver we have heard no more. That formidable seafaring man with one leg has gone clean out of my life, but I daresay he met his old Negress, and perhaps still lives in comfort with her and Captain Flint. It is to be hoped so, I suppose, for his chances of comfort in another world are very small.

The bar silver and the arms still lie, for all that I know, where Flint buried them; and certainly they shall lie there for me. Oxen and wain-ropes would not bring me back again to that accursed island; and the worst dreams that ever I have are when I hear the surf booming about its coasts or start upright in bed with the sharp voice of Captain Flint still ringing in my ears, "Pieces of eight! pieces of eight!"

Robert Louis Stevenson
(1850–1894)

AT AGE THIRTY-NINE, in Samoa, halfway around the world from his Scottish birthplace, Robert Louis Balfour Stevenson received the title that honored him the rest of his life: *Tusitala*, teller of tales. The fame of the author of *Treasure Island*, *Kidnapped*, and *The Strange Case of Dr. Jekyll and Mr. Hyde* had by then reached as far as his Samoan island home. But back in his childhood nursery in Edinburgh it would have been hard to imagine that the seeds of such a far-reaching and adventurous life were being sown.

Stevenson was born on November 13, 1850, into a family of civil engineers grown prominent as builders of Scotland's lighthouses. His mother was a high-spirited, graceful woman, with a zest for games and reading to her only child, but she suffered from the same weakness of the lungs that afflicted her son. At age two Stevenson had an attack of the croup that left him susceptible all his life to bronchitis, pneumonia, and eventually tuberculosis, and illness kept him out of regular schools until the age of nine.

Many nights when coughing kept the child awake, his father was at his bedside, diverting him with tales of ships and sailors and high adventure. Other times, in the arms of his nurse Cummie, he would look out at lighted windows in the distance, "where also, we told each other, there might be sick little boys and their nurses waiting, like us, for the morning." One of the author's most lasting books, *A Child's Garden of Verses*, bears the dedication to Alice Cunningham, the adored nurse, "from her boy."

Those feverish times and such a well-nourished imagination perhaps bred Stevenson's appetite for living life to the fullest whenever health allowed it. He was endowed as well with senses highly attuned to every sight and sound. In later years, remembering Edinburgh, Stevenson described

> the august airs of the castle on its rock, . . . the sudden song of the
> blackbird in the suburban lane, . . . the uninhabited splendors of the
> early dawn, the building up of the city on a misty day, house above

house, spire above spire, until it was received into a sky of softly glowing clouds.

A lover of words from the beginning, Stevenson customarily carried two books in his pockets, one to read and one to write in. For him the lack of traditional schooling may have been an asset, allowing his mind to wander where it would. At twelve, because of his mother's health, the family spent a winter on the French Riviera, and in the men's smoking lounges he visited with his father, Stevenson developed his gift for conversation and became at ease among strangers.

In 1867 he began his university training, supposedly to follow in his father's footsteps, but his boredom with engineering soon showed. On April 8, 1871, he declared to his father that he wanted to be a writer, and the carefully recorded date is probably a sign not only of the young man's conviction but also that the information was received as a blow. A compromise was struck, however, and Stevenson agreed to study law as preparation for a profession. Father and son remained close.

A long-boned and lean young man, Stevenson had warm brown eyes, a winning smile, and an eccentric disregard for appearances. In the era of the top hat and frock coat, his hair was unfashionably long, probably because illness forced it to go untended, and his favorite item of clothing earned him the nickname Velvet Coat. Never very interested in "polite" society, he preferred the companionship, he later wrote, of "seamen, chimney-sweeps, and thieves; my circle was being continually changed by the action of the police magistrate."

After passing the Scottish bar, Stevenson showed his enthusiasm for law by immediately setting off for France. Since early childhood he had written stories, plays, and essays, and produced his own magazines. Now he wrote in the styles of his favorite authors, to discover everything their wording might yield. Always polishing his language, he became master of a style that was later much admired by Henry James. In 1873 his essay "Roads" became the first article for which he was paid, but after 1877, when his first story appeared in print, his interest in fiction began to take precedence over the essays.

By that time Stevenson had met Fannie Osbourne, a dynamic, strong-minded, American woman eleven years his senior, at an artist's colony near Fontainebleau. Estranged from her husband, she had come to France with her teenage daughter and eight-year-old son to study painting. The two fell in love, but the situation was not promising, since Fannie was still married, and except for a family allowance, Stevenson had almost no money. In 1878 his first book appeared, about his travels in France. Fannie was back in California by then, and the following spring he received word that she was very ill. Against the advice of all his friends he set out for America, intending to marry her. He reached New York after a rough voyage aboard an immigrant ship. Two more weeks spent crossing the continent by train brought him to San Francisco in August, nearly dead.

For almost a year, before Fannie could marry, Stevenson lived and wrote in San Francisco and Monterey, often desperately lonely, without money, and terribly ill. Finally, the wedding took place in May. With Stevenson's new stepson, Lloyd Osbourne, the couple moved for a short while to a ghost town north of San Francisco, where they lived in abandoned buildings, an adventure recorded in *The Silverado Squatters*. Stevenson wrote later, "If I am where I am, it is thanks to the love of that lady, who married me when I was a mere complication of cough and bones, much fitter for an emblem of mortality than a bridegroom."

Returning to England, the threesome was lovingly received by Stevenson's parents, in spite of their disapproval of divorce. Because of Stevenson's lungs, they had to leave soon for the dry mountain air of Switzerland. The following year a treasure map drawn to entertain Lloyd inspired Stevenson to begin an adventure-filled tale called "The Sea-Cook," which was soon running in serialized form in a boys' magazine under the title *Treasure Island*. Paid twice what he had expected for its publication in book form, Stevenson set to work on *Kidnapped*, his imagination fired this time by a seaswept island off Scotland he had visited once.

Within the close circle of his family, Stevenson had the habit of reading his works aloud and taking the advice of his listeners. Eventually the family became more involved in his efforts, so that he wrote some of his stories, including "The Wrong Box," in collaboration with his stepson. On at least one occasion, the practice proved extremely trying, however: when Fannie did not like *The Strange Case of Dr. Jekyll and Mr. Hyde* on first hearing, and said her husband had merely written a thriller. After an angry exchange Stevenson left the room, but later threw the manuscript into the fire, admitting his wife was right. He wrote a new version, deepening the story's meaning, and it became a great success.

Still seeking a place where he could be healthy, the family set out in 1887 for the United States, where it became evident that *Treasure Island* and *Dr. Jekyll and Mr. Hyde* had made Stevenson famous. After a winter in upstate New York, during which Stevenson was under a doctor's care, Fannie headed to the West Coast to charter a yacht. For the next three years, Stevenson cruised the Pacific with his wife, stepson, and widowed mother, writing articles and regaining his health.

Stevenson missed Europe, but the South Pacific islands of Samoa seemed the sensible place to settle. Shipping routes made it one of the few places in that part of the world where mail service was dependable, and on the author's 400-acre estate carved out of the island jungle, he lived and worked virtually free of illness for the first time in his life.

At forty-four, Stevenson was struck down suddenly, not by tuberculosis but by a cerebral hemorrhage. He had forged strong friendships among the Samoan chieftains, and within hours they had gathered forty natives, who worked through the night cutting a path up Mount Vaea to the author's chosen grave site, and then bore his coffin to its resting place, in homage to their beloved *Tusitala*.

Other Titles by Robert Louis Stevenson

The Black Arrow. New York: Scribner's, 1987.

A Child's Garden of Verses. New York: Macmillan, 1981.

Dr. Jekyll and Mr. Hyde. New York: Bantam, 1981.

The Master of Ballantrae. Emma Letly, editor. New York: Oxford University Press, 1983.

The Moon. New York: Harper & Row, 1984.

The New Arabian Nights. Boston: Shambhala, 1986.

Travels With a Donkey; An Inland Voyage; The Silverado Squatters. Totowa, NJ: Biblio, 1978.

Weir of Hermiston & Other Stories. Paul Binding, editor. New York: Penguin, 1980.

The Wrong Box. London: Amereon, 1979.